Lake 40

Beth Connor

Wolf Grove Media, LLC

1st edition 2024

PRINT: ISBN: 978-1-958329-21-4

EBOOK: ISBN: 978-1-958329-22-1

This ones for you, Steve, for your unwavering support and endless encouragement. Your belief in me has been my greatest source of strength. Thank you for always standing by my side and inspiring me to reach for my dreams.

Prologue

The subsequent entries have been transcribed verbatim from a journal discovered just off the Lake 40 trail in (redacted), Washington, USA. Its contents provide a first-hand account of a series of events in the summer of 2019, detailing the author's explorations into obscure rituals and the alleged supernatural. The authenticity of the experiences and the identity of the journal's author remain unknown. Readers are advised to approach with an open mind, recognizing the blurred line between reality and fiction that often accompanies such discoveries.

Journal Entry: June 1, 2019

Tried 'The Fade' tonight. I had all the mirrors set up, following the steps exactly as described. Wasn't entirely sure what to expect, but the folks on the subreddit seem pretty intrigued by it.

At first, nothing happened, but when I checked the time, nearly an hour had passed. I don't remember spacing out, and that gnawing feeling of something just beyond my grasp is unsettling. Need to think about this. Will write more later.

Journal Entry: June 5, 2019

The Fade was... weird? Didn't quite get the profound experience some others claimed, but there were moments over the last few days where I felt an inexplicable chill, as if eyes were tracking my every move.

Journal Entry: June 8, 2019

Stumbled upon another one of those urban legend 'games.' Thinking of giving this a shot tomorrow night after work. It involves another candle, a dark room, and whispered chants. I mean, what's the worst that could happen, right? There's a strange thrill in not knowing.

Journal Entry: June 14, 2019

Okay, the candle game was a bust. Nothing happened. Maybe it's just my skeptical mind, but there's a lingering question: what if there's some truth hidden in these legends?

Journal Entry: June 20, 2019

A friend told me about a local ritual, but this one's outside. A solo hike at midnight called the 'Lake 40 Challenge.' Initially brushed it off. I'm not much of a hiker, but there's something about it that's nagging at me. The idea of a night hike, combined with the potential for something otherworldly, is irresistibly intriguing.

Journal Entry: June 23, 2019

Prepping for the 'Lake 40 Challenge.' Got a headlamp, poles, and some safety gear. I'm genuinely excited. Even if I don't encounter anything supernatural, I'm sure it'll be a memorable experience. A few folks on the subreddit mentioned it too, so it's gained some traction.

Journal Entry: June 27, 2019

Two days out from the 'Lake 40 Challenge.' Re-read the ritual steps. I'm not a superstitious person, but there's this nagging feeling I can't shake off. Maybe it's the allure of the unknown? Either way, I'm committed now. Let's see how this goes.

Journal Entry: June 30, 2019

Had everything prepared to do the 'Lake 40 Challenge,' but my friend, who was supposed to drop me off, bailed last minute. A bit frustrating, but maybe it's a sign? Going to reschedule it for another night. Just for clarity, jotting down the ritual steps again:

The Lake 40 Challenge:

　　1. *Start your hike at the Lake 40 Trailhead at midnight on a moonless night. Be alone. If there's a car*

in the lot or people around, do not proceed.

2. *Walk steadily and don't look back. If you hear noises or voices behind you, ignore them.*

3. *Past the 1.3-mile marker, find a moss-covered rock with a crack. Put a personal item inside. Stay focused on the rock and trail.*

4. *At the lake, sit facing the water. Close your eyes and listen. If you don't hear a baby's cry, the ritual failed.*

5. *If you hear the cry, look into the water. Keep your gaze steady even if you see shapes or hear whispers.*

6. *If a dark figure appears, you've succeeded. Avoid its eyes and don't answer its questions.*

7. *Regardless of the result, leave without looking back or taking your item. Following these steps will grant you the sight, revealing hidden paths.*

8. *Never share your experience. Speaking of it attracts unwelcome attention from the fade.*

I'll need to set a new date soon. The anticipation is building.

Journal Entry: July 1, 2019

Checked the lunar calendar today. The next new moon is on July 2nd, but with the upcoming festivities, I don't want to risk it. Rescheduled for the next new moon on July 31st. I've got this feeling that July 31st is going to be the perfect night for this. The wait will be worth it.

Journal Entry: July 10, 2019

Did a dry run today, in broad daylight, of course. Located the 1.3-mile marker and found the moss-covered rock with a prominent crack. Even during the day, the place felt heavy, like the air was thick with whispers of the past. Regardless, I'm feeling more prepared.

Journal Entry: July 20, 2019

Ever since my recon trip, I've had peculiar dreams. Visions of moonlit lakes, dark figures lurking just beyond my sight, and eerie lullabies. I wake up feeling like I've genuinely been somewhere else. Maybe it's just nerves, but it feels like something is reaching out to me.

Journal Entry: July 23, 2019

Second thoughts about using grandpa's watch. It holds too much sentimental value. Instead, thought about using this journal. Leaving behind a record of my thoughts feels more personal. If the offering needs to be a piece of oneself, this journal might be perfect.

Journal Entry: July 28, 2019

News broke today about a body found near the Lake 40 Trailhead. They're calling it a bear attack, but the rumors are flying. My imagination isn't helping. Is this related to the 'Lake 40 Challenge'? The thought sends a shiver down my spine.

Journal Entry: July 30, 2019

The day has been dragging. Friends warned me about nocturnal hikes, and their words weigh heavily. Revisited the ritual steps. Every rustle outside makes me jump. There's a thickness in the air, an electric charge. The night feels alive with anticipation.

Journal Entry: July 31, 2019

Well, tonight's the big night. I've got a weird mix of nerves and excitement churning in my stomach. Going through the ritual steps one more time, just to make sure I've got everything down. Can't shake off the thought of that bear attack, though; nature has its own dangers, even with no added supernatural elements. Still, I've come this far, and I'm too curious to back down now. If, for some wild reason, I don't make it back, I hope this journal finds its way to someone. It's been an interesting ride documenting all of this. Guess we'll see how tonight turns out. Catch you on the flip side!

CHAPTER 1

October 15, 2019

Darkness hung heavy over the misty trailhead, an unwelcome shroud for the horror that lay beneath. The neon orange police tape glowed like a sinister beacon, marking the entrance to a nightmare. Detective Dominique 'Dom' Dupont stood at the edge with the past pressing against him. Another body had been found here back in July, supposedly because of a bear attack, though Dom had his doubts. It seemed this trailhead was collecting bodies.

"Everett was supposed to be a fresh start, huh?" Lauren Kim, Dom's pint-sized partner, muttered as she approached, her eyes fixed on the gruesome scene before them. "Now we're dealing with some freaky ritual site."

"Yeah, and it's not the first time. Remember the body they found here in July? They blamed it on a bear attack, but something didn't add up."

Dom remained silent. He knew better than to dismiss the strange and unexplained. His spiritual upbringing had taught him that the world was far more complex than most believed. As he surveyed the scene, the mist clung to the ground like a living entity, the air thick with tension.

He had left New Orleans to escape memories that tailed him like shadows—days filled with supernatural cases that defied logic and nights haunted by dreams of things best left unseen. But the ghosts of the past had a way of following, no matter how far he ran.

"Have you heard of the Lake 40 challenge?" Lauren asked, glancing at the scene again. Dom could see the nervousness in her eyes, but her determination would never let her back down.

He shook his head, his jaw tight. It sounded like one of those local legends that people whispered about, a dark urban myth promising otherworldly experiences if only one dared to step through the veil. He knew from experience it was something you just don't mess with without a plan.

As Dom looked at the site before him, he couldn't help but feel the crossroads calling to him. He could sense the connection to the other side, the pull of the unseen.

Lauren shifted, her eyes scanning the scene, searching for something—anything—to make sense of the horror before them. "We're going to need some serious help with this one, Dom," she admitted.

A crime scene tech nearby overheard and chimed in, "This is right up your alley, Dupont."

Dom felt a twinge of irritation. "What's that supposed to mean?"

The tech shrugged, a slight smirk on his face. "You know, with your reputation for solving the... unusual cases."

Dom bristled at the comment but kept his face neutral. His reputation for handling cases involving the supernatural had followed him from New Orleans to Everett, and it was something he had never been comfortable with. The strange cases seemed to find him, and while he didn't seek them out, he couldn't deny that he had a knack for them. But he hated the idea that his colleagues saw him as some kind of paranormal expert.

Lauren noticed the exchange and redirected. "Alright, let's focus on the task at hand. Dom, what do you make of this?"

He didn't respond, his eyes locked on the lifeless area, the police tape, and the dark trail that seemed to stretch into oblivion. He knew that in the shadows, something terrible had been awakened, human or beyond. And it was up to them to confront it.

A lone car approached the desolate road, its headlights cutting through the mist like a knife. This late in the season, the campers had dwindled to a few die-hard hikers, determined to wring every moment from the damp wilderness.

Dom's eyes swept over the surroundings. Everything was chaos. Blood and viscera from rodents and forest creatures lay in a gruesome circle, as if something had torn them to shreds. It was like the scene back in July. Someone had made an anonymous tip about a crime here; when the ranger investigated, he had found this scene. The initial assessment was that it was an animal attack, but Dom wasn't so sure.

Lauren grimaced at the sight. "Dom, what animal could have done this? I mean, the ground in the middle is clean, but everything around it is just... destroyed."

Her voice trailed off, her eyes darting around the macabre scene, searching for any explanation. Dom felt that familiar sensation urging him to look deeper, to see the unseen. But he fought the urge, knowing that revealing his connection to the other side would only bring more questions and fear.

"Lets look at this from every angle," Dom replied, his voice steady as he surveyed the unsettling juxtaposition of peace and violence.

"Okay, widen the perimeter and secure the scene," Lauren instructed, directing a handful of officers and crime scene techs to assist them.

As the team worked, Lauren took photographs, capturing every angle and detail for later analysis. Dom, meanwhile, slipped on a pair of latex gloves and examined the area.

He noticed something odd about the way the shredded creatures were scattered. The pattern seemed almost deliberate, as if someone—or something—had placed them there with a purpose. The arrangement made his skin crawl.

Lauren, having finished her photography, joined him. "Let's take a walk up the path a bit," she suggested, her voice subdued. "Maybe there's something that can help us understand what might have happened."

It still wasn't even clear if this was an actual crime scene. All they had to go on was an anonymous tip. For all they knew, it *was* an animal attack. But Dom knew. He could feel it in his bones. The moon hid behind heavy clouds and the trailhead was hard to see. The occasional sweep of headlights what the only thing that broke the darkness. A chill hung in the air as Dom and Lauren stepped onto the path, the single beam of light from their flashlights making their breath visible in the chilly October air.

As they followed the trail, Dom couldn't shake the memories of his early days as a beat cop in New Orleans. Back then, his instincts—the ones that had earned him a fast track to detective—had saved his skin more times than he could count. That same sixth sense was tingling now, warning him that something was off. He'd moved up here to escape the strange and unexplainable cases that seemed to haunt him, but it was clear they had followed him to the Pacific Northwest.

Lauren's voice broke through his reverie. "Dom, do you think we might find something supernatural out here? I mean, isn't it possible that this is just some sick prank?"

Dom shook his head. "I wish it were that simple. There's something about this place, about the way the air feels… it's too similar to what I've seen before."

Lauren fell silent, her face a mask of concentration. Dom knew she was struggling with her own demons. Her relationship with her girlfriend Natalie had been deteriorating for months, and the stress was taking its toll. She had confided in him once, after a nasty fight, her voice breaking as she admitted how trapped she felt. It was a side of her she rarely showed, preferring to keep up the facade of strength and determination.

They continued down the trail, and Lauren's keen eyes caught something unusual. She stopped, pointing to the ground. "Dom, look at this."

There, in the damp earth, were a series of footprints, some larger than others, leading further into the woods. The underbrush had been trampled and broken, suggesting that someone—or something—had passed through.

"Maybe this isn't supernatural after all," Lauren mused hopefully, examining the footprints more closely. "It could be the work of a human, or even a wild animal."

Dom crouched down beside her, studying the tracks. He still felt like something more was at play here. But they couldn't dismiss the possibility of a more mundane explanation just yet. "We should follow these tracks," he said, straightening up. "See where they lead. Stay alert."

Dom and Lauren followed the tracks deeper into the woods, but they came to an abrupt halt when the footprints stopped, leaving no sign of their quarry. They exchanged puzzled glances as the eerie atmosphere settled around them like a heavy fog.

"This doesn't make any sense," Lauren whispered. "How can the tracks just... stop like this?"

Dom frowned, scanning the area for any further clues. But there was nothing—no broken branches, no disturbed earth, nothing to suggest where the trail might have continued. It was as if whatever had made the tracks had vanished.

"Let's head back to the station," Dom suggested, his voice tight with frustration. "It's dark, and we're going to miss stuff. We can regroup there, try to piece together what we've found so far, and figure out our next move."

Lauren nodded, and the two detectives retraced their steps back to the trailhead. As they made their way through the dark forest, the unsettling quiet and the lingering sense of unease followed them like a specter they couldn't shake. The trees, their twisted branches like skeletal fingers, seemed to close in on them, casting elongated shadows that danced in the faint light of their flashlights.

As they continued backtracking, Lauren spotted something. "Hold on, Dom," she said, pointing toward a mossy rock with something sticking out of a crack. They approached it. A dirty, wet journal was wedged into the rock. Dom bagged it. "We'll look at this more at the station," he said, marking the spot. The journal's presence, combined with the bizarre scene, hinted at a connection. Lauren jotted down the location in her notes, her hands trembling as the silence pressed in around them.

After walking a while, Lauren commented, "It didn't seem like we walked this far coming in." The trees seemed denser, the path less familiar. An eerie silence enveloped them, broken only by their footsteps and the occasional rustle of leaves. The air grew colder, the temperature dropping, causing their breath to mist in the dim light.

Dom glanced around. "It's like the forest is... changing," he muttered. The path ahead seemed to twist and turn in ways it hadn't before, and a creeping sense of dread coiled around his thoughts.

The wind picked up, carrying with it a faint, almost imperceptible whisper that sounded like a woman calling for help. Dom stopped in his tracks, straining to catch the elusive sound. "Did you hear that?" he asked, his voice tight with unease.

Lauren shook her head, but her eyes darted around the shadowy woods. "No, but I feel like we're being watched."

Dom struggled with himself, torn between his instinct to help someone in trouble and the nagging doubt that it might be all in his imagination. If someone needed help, he couldn't ignore it, but if Lauren heard nothing, maybe it was just his mind playing tricks on him.

The forest seemed to close in around them; trees pressing closer. The path twisted into an ominous labyrinth, each step leading them deeper into the unknown. Shadows danced in the corners of their vision.

Dom's pulse quickened. He knew this feeling, a sensation that tugged at his memories of a place his mémère had often warned him about. "Lets keep moving," he urged, though his legs felt leaden. Every step seemed to echo in the silence, a reminder of how alone they were.

A branch snapped behind them. Both Lauren and Dom whipped around, eyes wide, searching for the source of the noise. There was nothing but darkness and the vague outline of trees, yet the feeling of being watched made Dom's skin prickle like static electricity.

"Hurry," Lauren whispered, her voice trembling.

They quickened their pace, the sound of their footsteps merging into a rapid, syncopated rhythm. The path twisted more sharply now, each turn revealing more of the forest's dark heart. The trees seemed to whisper secrets to one another, their rustling leaves a sinister backdrop for their escape.

Just when panic set in, Dom heard the distant voices of the techs at the scene ahead. The familiar sounds brought a wave of relief, but the unsettling feeling lingered. It was as if the forest had claimed them, only to release them back to reality.

"Let's get out of here," Dom said, his voice tense.

Lauren's gaze lingered on the shadowy forest behind them. "Yeah," she replied. "Something about this place feels... wrong."

As they stepped past the tape, the oppressive atmosphere lifted slightly, yet the haunting presence of the forest lingered. Whatever they had encountered on that twisted path had left a lasting impression on their minds. The journal in their possession seemed to pulse with ominous energy, offering more questions than answers. The forest shadows, however, seemed to whisper a promise: they would return, and next time, the forest might not let them go.

Back at the station, Dom spread out his notes and photographs, documenting the patterns of the carcasses and each marking carved into trees and rocks. The scene tugged at the edges of his memory, hinting at a knowledge buried deep within his past.

Lauren stood beside him, her own notes scattered across the desk. "These symbols carved into the trees... Do you think they have anything to do with the crime scene?"

"Possibly," Dom replied, his voice thoughtful. "Or they could be part of something older."

"I'll start digging through the local archives, see if there's any mention of similar markings," Lauren replied. "Maybe we'll find a connection."

As Lauren busied herself with the research, Dom tried to focus on the investigation, but the unsettling presence he'd felt earlier lingered. He kept the sensation to himself, knowing it would only raise more questions. He couldn't afford distractions—not now, when the darkness seemed to close in from all sides.

CHAPTER 2

June 1, 2019

School's out, and my roommates have scattered—some fleeing home for the summer, others working overtime to pay the bills. But not me. I'm staying, and determined to finish the summer semester. Just two more classes, and I'll have my AA. My mom will be happy, not that she cares. To her, community college reflects poorly on the family. Straight A's and a doctorate in the sciences are her expectations.

Both my parents scoff at anything mystical or paranormal. Dad calls it 'nonsense,' and Mom shakes her head, urging me to focus on 'real' knowledge. But I love it. There's something thrilling about the unknown, about rituals and the possibility of something beyond the everyday grind. Living on my own, roommates aside, gives me the freedom to explore my fascination.

I open my laptop and click on the Reddit link. Taylor was supposed to be here, but she bailed. She said this stuff freaks her out. Typical.

The screen glows with the title: "The Fade Ritual—Instructions." My heart beats faster. I skim the steps as a quick reminder:

- Set up mirrors in a triangular formation around you. Make sure they all face inward, reflecting each other.

- Place a lit candle in the center of the triangle.

- Sit down in the middle of the triangle and close your eyes.

- Recite the incantation three times: "Into the Fade, I go. Beyond the veil, show me what I need to know."

- Keep your eyes closed and wait. You should feel a presence or see visions in your mind.

Three old mirrors from around the apartment—each with its own history: a gilded frame, a plain rectangle, and a small, round hand mirror. The gilded frame mirror is my favorite, 'borrowed' from the common room. Its elaborate design always catches my eye. The plain rectangular one is from my bathroom, utilitarian but reliable. The small, round hand mirror belongs to one of my roommates, who wouldn't miss it over the summer. Arranging them into a triangle on the floor, their reflective surfaces face each other, creating an eerie labyrinth of reflections. The air feels electric, like the moments before a storm.

I light the candle and place it at the center of the triangle. The flame dances, casting strange, shifting shadows on the walls. Sitting cross-legged in the middle, I feel the distant gaze of the mirrors on my skin. 'Into the Fade, I go. Beyond the veil, show me what I need to know.' My voice wavers, a whisper against the oppressive silence. By the third recitation, my breath hitches. The words barely escape my lips over the pounding of my heart.

Time slows, and I wait. The seconds stretch out, each one longer than the last. Outside my window, the sound of cars passing breaks the silence. I should have shut it. *Focus!*

The ritual doesn't specify what is supposed to happen next, just promises "a presence or visions." The ambiguity leaves my mind to wander, picking up on every minor detail. A spider crawls up the wall, its tiny legs moving. I pretend I can hear its footsteps, imagining the faintest of taps against the peeling paint.

So much hope rests on this one—more than I care to admit. The excitement of the unknown, the thrill that this time might be different. But as the minutes tick by, doubt creeps in.

Another ritual, another disappointment. The familiar feeling of letdown sinks in. Why do I keep falling for this stuff? Yet, I can't help but chase the thrill, the sliver of hope that one day, something extraordinary will happen.

The room remains still, the candle flame steady. I unclench my fists and let out a long sigh. Maybe I'll try another ritual tomorrow. Or maybe I'll give it a rest. But deep down, I know I'll never really stop. The allure of the unknown is too strong. My watch says 11:30. That's strange. It was before 9 when I started. Intriguing. Maybe something happened. The concept of lost time is fascinating and unsettling. Did I enter some sort of trance? Did I experience something beyond my conscious awareness?

I should record these sessions. A video camera, maybe even a microphone to capture any anomalies or changes. I can't keep relying on my memory. If I want to take this seriously, I need evidence. Proof that something, anything, is happening.

Determined, I make a mental note to gather the equipment. This isn't over. Far from it. The lost time might be the breakthrough I've been waiting for, a sign that I'm on the right path. Next time, I'll be prepared to catch whatever happens.

Before I open my laptop, I grab my notation journal. It's a pretty thing my friend Taylor got me for my birthday.

The cover is a deep blue, with intricate silver designs that shimmer when they catch the light. It has a soft, almost velvety texture, and the pages are thick and creamy, inviting ink to flow across them. A small silver clasp keeps it shut, and a matching ribbon marker helps me keep my place.

Most people don't see me—not in an actual invisible sort of way. They just see a brainy Asian girl who doesn't talk. I blend into the background, unnoticed, unremarkable. But Taylor sees more. She looks past the quiet exterior and understands the thoughts and curiosities that make up my world. She knows the inner workings of my mind better than anyone, including my parents.

When she gave me the journal, she said it reminded her of me—beautiful but mysterious. I can still see the sparkle in her eyes and the sincere smile on her face. For her, this wasn't just a gift; it was a way to say she saw me, the real me, and she valued that, and I value her.

This journal is where I capture my surface thoughts, my experiments, and my observations. It's not for personal confessions, but for documenting the strange and the unexplained. It's a place where I can be honest about my passion without fear of judgment.

As I run my fingers over the cover, I feel a connection to Taylor that goes beyond friendship. She's my confidante in this journey, even if she doesn't share my obsession. She gives me a sense of belonging, a reminder that someone sees the real me and accepts me as I am. There is only one other person in the world I can say that about: Luke, better known by his Discord username, Ardent Elan.

We met on a subreddit about lucid dreaming and just hit it off. I had met no one as interested in this stuff as I was until I met Luke. He is usually on the Discord server he runs called Mystic Realms, a place where people can discuss their trials with stuff like this. I hope he is online now—I could use his thoughts on this Fade ritual.

My laptop is old. I've got duct tape on the side near the power source because it cracked once when I dropped it. I try to be patient and run to the kitchen to grab a snack while it boots up. The veggie straws melt in my mouth as I type him a DM.

DreamSeeker: Hey, you there?

ArdentElan: Hey! What's up?

DreamSeeker: I need to share something that happened during my latest session—the Fade thing you linked me. It's kinda freaky.

ArdentElan: I'm all ears. What happened?

DreamSeeker: I was trying the ritual. Everything was fine, but nothing happened. But then... I lost time.

ArdentElan: Lost time? Like you blacked out?

DreamSeeker: Sort of. One moment I was following the ritual, trying to focus and not be bored out of my mind. Then I just gave up. But here's the weird part—

ArdentElan: There's always a weird part, isn't there?

DreamSeeker: I checked my watch, and almost two hours had passed. It felt like only minutes to me.

ArdentElan: That's really strange. Have you experienced anything like this before?

DreamSeeker: Not to this extent. I've had some fuzzy memories, but never complete blackouts with lost time.

ArdentElan: Did you notice anything unusual? Physical sensations, objects out of place, anything at all?

DreamSeeker: Not really. The room was colder than usual, and I had this weird, heavy feeling, I guess.

ArdentElan: Interesting. The cold could indicate some sort of energy shift. Did you document everything? Write it all down?

DreamSeeker: Yeah, I wrote a bit in my journal. It's all there, every detail I can remember. I usually write more after a sleep.

ArdentElan: Good. Keep doing that. Do you think you might try this one again?

DreamSeeker: I'm not sure. What do you think?

Ardent Elan: I think so. Maybe take a break and try to understand what happened before attempting it again. We can analyze your notes together.

DreamSeeker: I'd like that. Thanks, Luke. I always feel better after talking to you.

ArdentElan: Anytime. Stay safe and keep me posted on any developments.

DreamSeeker: Will do. Talk to you later."

ArdentElan: "Hey, before you go... do you want to try meeting up again tonight?

DreamSeeker: Yeah, I'd like that. Where should we meet this time?

ArdentElan: How about the Statue of Liberty?

DreamSeeker: Perfect. See you in the dreamworld.

ArdentElan: See you there. Take care.

Luke and I like to meet when we are lucid dreaming. We both have experimented with out-of-body experiences, despite knowing the risks. It's supposed to be dangerous because you never know what might jump into your body while you're not occupying it. But the thrill of the unknown, the possibility of connecting in such an extraordinary way, keeps us coming back.

We always choose a place we both know well, somewhere familiar to both of us. He lives pretty far away, in Florida, but our shared passion for the mystical and paranormal has created a bond. We've tried meeting in places like Central Park, the beach at Miami, and the Grand Canyon—all dreamscapes where our minds can meet when our bodies can't.

Tonight, we've chosen the Statue of Liberty. It's a place we've both visited in the waking world. I close my laptop, my thoughts already drifting toward tonight's attempt. The anticipation is a mix of excitement and a touch of fear. What if the lost time I experienced earlier is a sign of something more? What if it happens again?

As I settle into bed, I set my intention and do a quick meditation. Then I reaffirm a commitment to exploring the unknown, no matter the risks. Tonight, I'll be ready and hope Luke will be, too.

CHAPTER 3

October 16, 2019

It was after midnight when they arrived back at the station. Dom and Lauren sat at a cluttered desk under harsh fluorescent lights. The station, far removed from the eerie forest, still carried a sense of unease that had followed them. Dom removed the journal from the evidence bag, its damp pages sticking together. He felt an inexplicable pull toward the journal, as if it contained answers just beyond his reach. His mémère always said objects have power—especially personal ones. What did this journal mean, and why was he so drawn to it?

"We need to dry this out before we can make any sense of it," Lauren said, breaking the silence. She disappeared into the locker room and returned moments later with a hair dryer. As she dried the journal's pages, Dom's mind raced with the implications of what they might find.

Lauren leaned in, her eyes scanning the first few pages. "Looks like someone's diary," she murmured, her finger tracing the faint, water-damaged writing, then handed it to him.

Dom picked up the journal, feeling its weight in his hands. Its cover was a deep blue with intricate silver designs that shimmered under the harsh lights. An artifact from another world. The journal seemed out of place here. The thick, creamy pages were now warped from moisture. A small silver clasp had kept it shut, and a matching ribbon marker, frayed, hinted at frequent use.

He flipped through the damp pages, his eyes catching snippets of entries about rituals, strange sightings, and mentions of the Lake 40 Challenge.

"The writing's legible," Lauren noted, her voice a mix of relief and curiosity. "Dated too—that's always convenient."

Dom turned the pages, observing the minimal details. This person had things to say, but they held back. It seemed more like an outline of documentation than real diary entries.

"Look." he held the book out to Lauren. "The Lake 40 Challenge. Didn't you mention that, too?"

"Its local lore. Not sure I remember it from my child-hood. I think it came about more when that elevator game thingie got press. I imagine someone made it up."

Dom took it all in. Even made-up things had pow-er. How many people had done this ritual since it had been created? What spirit had latched onto the power? He shook his head. This was his Mémère talking, not him.

"Lauren, why do you think someone would create a challenge like the Lake 40?" Dom asked.

"Maybe it started as a dare or a test of courage. But with rituals like these, they take on a life of their own. People believe in the power they hold, and that belief can make them real," Lauren replied. "Let's hold off on drawing conclusions until we have more context."

"Agreed."

A knock on the door interrupted them. Detective Jones, a burly man with a no-nonsense attitude, entered. "Got the preliminary reports from the scene," he said, handing Dom a folder. "Looks like animal blood. No human re-mains. But there's something off about the samples—lab techs are still running tests."

Dom took the folder. "Thanks, Jones. Let us know as soon as they find anything concrete."

Jones glanced at the journal on the desk and smirked. "You really think some spooky journal is gonna crack this case wide open?" he chuckled.

Dom's frustration rose and he forced a tight smile. "We're looking at all angles, Jones. Every clue helps."

Jones shrugged and left the room. Dom's thoughts churned. He knew the skepticism all too well but couldn't ignore his instincts. The strange cases had a way of revealing truths that logic couldn't grasp, and he had learned to trust his gut.

"We need to connect the dots between this journal and what we found out there. Someone is trying to summon something—or communicate with something—let's see if any recent missing persons cases line up with what we've found." Dom told Lauren.

Lauren's phone buzzed, breaking the silence. She glanced at the screen and groaned. "It's Natalie," she muttered, stepping outside to take the call.

Dom watched her go, his mind churning with thoughts. He knew Lauren was struggling with her personal life, but she was strong—stronger than she gave herself credit for. He just hoped she could hold it together long enough to solve this case.

He turned his attention back to the journal, flipping through the pages. The text was minimal, but the intent was clear: someone was trying to reach the other side.

Dom's thoughts drifted back to New Orleans, to the nights he'd spent chasing shadows and confronting things that shouldn't exist. He'd moved here to escape that life, but it seemed it had found him again. The forest, the ritual site, the journal—they were all pieces of a puzzle that was becoming all too familiar.

Lauren returned, her face pale and strained. "Natalie is drunk again," she breathed. "She's yelling about God knows what. I told her I'm working, but…"

Dom reached out, placing a reassuring hand on her shoulder. "You'll get through this, Lauren. Do you need to go get her?"

"No," Lauren sighed. "Pete got her a cab."

"Who's Pete?" Dom asked.

Lauren's face reddened. "The bartender."

"Let's focus on the case for now."

Lauren agreed, taking a deep breath. "You're right." They focused on reports around the Mount Pilchuck area. Granite Falls had a lot of missing persons cases, although most had to do with boating accidents. It was a strange mix of small-town locals and outdoor enthusiasts. Time slipped by as they scoured through reports, each recent case adding to the mystery and dread.

Frustration mounted until Lauren's eyes widened at the screen. "Dom, look at this," she said, her voice tinged with excitement.

It was the case of Everett, WA resident Lily Chen, reported missing in August after going on a hike in the Pilchuck area. Dom felt a chill run down his spine. His sixth sense knew this was the case. "This is it," he said. "Let's dig deeper."

The details of Lily's case were familiar. Local girl, reported missing by a friend. Apparently, the friend had dropped her off for a late-night solo backpacking trip, planning to pick her up the next day. When she returned, Lily was not there. She waited and reported it to the ranger, who then got the police involved. The case was still open because her parents refused to close it, but the notes said it was an animal attack, as there had been another recent bear attack, and the animal had not been captured and euthanized yet. The strange circumstances of her disappearance mirrored the eerie sense of foreboding that had haunted them since they found the journal.

Dom and Lauren exchanged a look.

"Lets get this journal analyzed, maybe reach out to the friend to see if it's Lily's," Dom said, his voice resolute. "It could connect it to her case."

Lauren's gaze lingered on the journal. "And we need to visit her family, see if they can tell us anything that wasn't in the report."

"Hey—it's after 3," Dom said. "You need to get some sleep and go take care of Natalie."

Lauren frowned, her expression tired and worried. "She's already passed out," she replied, rubbing her temples. "But you're right. My brain is going in circles." She paused, then added, "I'll text you when I wake up, and we can go see the family and friends of this Lily Chen case."

"Done," Dom said, giving her a reassuring nod.

As Lauren gathered her things, Dom couldn't help but notice the weariness in her movements. She had been pushing herself hard, and it was taking its toll. He watched her leave, the case still stuck in his head. The station's fluorescent lights flickered, casting shadows that seemed to dance along the walls, a haunting reminder of the night's events.

Once Lauren was gone, Dom allowed himself a moment of reflection. He brushed a hand over the coarse stubble on his jaw, the exhaustion in his bones becoming impossible to ignore.

The journal, still open on the desk, seemed to beckon him with its mysteries. He knew he should get some rest too, but the pull of the unknown was too strong.

He sat back down, eyes scanning the cryptic entries once more. The intricate designs on the cover, the meticulous handwriting—it all hinted at something far deeper than a mere diary. Dom's mind wandered to his past, the cases he'd worked on in New Orleans, the things he'd seen that defied explanation.

The silence of the station was almost oppressive, broken only by the faint hum of machinery and the distant ticking of a clock. Dom felt a shiver run down his spine, the hairs on the back of his neck standing up.

With a deep sigh, Dom closed the journal and stood up. He needed to rest as well, to clear his mind. As he made his way to his car, the cool night air was a welcome contrast to the stifling atmosphere of the station. The drive home was a blur, his thoughts consumed by the case and the strange sense of foreboding that seemed to cling to him.

Dom navigated the empty streets, the quiet hum of the engine his only companion. His mind churned with thoughts of the case, the journal, and the unknown forces at play. Streetlights cast shadows on the pavement, mirroring the shadows of doubt and fear in his mind. Every corner he turned seemed to bring a fresh wave of unease, as if the darkness itself were closing in around him.

He knew that sleep would be elusive, but he couldn't help himself. The case had awakened a part of him he had kept hidden, memories of past encounters with the supernatural resurfacing with a vengeance. Incense from his Mémère's rituals, the hushed whispers of old New Orleans streets, the unexplainable phenomena he had witnessed—all of it came rushing back. Now, it seemed, there was no turning back.

Dom thought of the journal and its entries. He couldn't shake the feeling that it was a key to something much larger, something that transcended the mundane details of their investigation. It both intrigued and unnerved him.

As he approached his place, the familiar sight did little to soothe his troubled mind. He parked the car and sat for a moment, the engine ticking as it cooled. The quiet suburban street seemed worlds away from the dark, twisted path they had walked in the forest, yet the sense of foreboding followed him like a shadow.

Dom stepped out of the car, the cool night air hitting his face and bringing a momentary clarity. He made his way to the front door, his footsteps echoing in the stillness. Inside, the house was dark and silent, a stark contrast to the turmoil in his mind.

He dropped his keys on the counter and glanced at the clock. It was late. Dom rubbed a hand over his stubble, feeling the exhaustion settle deep into his bones. Despite the weariness, his mind refused to quiet. He knew he needed rest, but the mysteries kept gnawing at him.

Now his head was spinning. He pulled out a chair in front of his computer and stared at the screen as it booted up. He was exhausted—he knew that. But sleep would not come until he let all this play out in his mind.

Dom had always felt a connection to the supernatural, something he rarely admitted. His Mémère had been a spiritual healer in New Orleans, and she had taught him to see beyond the physical world. He had tried to leave that part of his life behind, but cases like Lily's brought it all rushing back.

His mind drifted back to a sweltering summer in New Orleans. He stood in a small, dimly lit room, the air thick. A woman's lifeless body lay on the floor, strange symbols carved into her skin. The locals spoke in hushed tones about "opening the door," a ritual that was said to let spirits cross into the living world. Dom had never proved the supernatural elements of that case, but the eerie parallels to Lily's disappearance were impossible to ignore.

He couldn't help but think of his partner. Lauren had seen glimpses of his otherworldly intuition, but he had never explained it to her. The supernatural was not something easy to share or understand. He knew she was curious, perhaps even a little frightened, but her determination to find the truth kept her grounded.

He opened a browser window and typed in "Lake 40 Challenge." A few Reddit links to urban legends came up, along with links to some PNW creepy-stuff podcasts and basic info on the trail and the hike, but there wasn't a lot to go off. He clicked on one subreddit and found the same instructions that were written in the journal. He was about to give up, but then he searched for bear attacks near the Lake 40 trail. This brought up something odd.

His eyes widened as he read through the peculiar details of the bear attacks in the area. Survivors described feeling an unnatural coldness and hearing whispers just before the attacks. One report mentioned a hiker who had seen a shadowy figure lurking nearby moments before. Another survivor finding a strange marking on his body, as if he had been marked by something—or someone. Not one of them remembered seeing the bear.

Dom dug deeper, finding archived information on an obscure local history website. The site hosted digitized copies of old newspaper clippings and historical records. Dom's heart raced as he delved deeper into the history of the area. An article from the 1920s detailed a series of mysterious animal attacks, similar to the recent ones. These historical accounts often mentioned local rituals and challenges.

In the summer of 1923, several local farmers reported seeing strange lights near Lake 40. Shortly after, livestock began disappearing, and the bodies that were found bore strange symbols etched into their flesh.

The articles described how these attacks often coincided with local legends and rituals, similar to the Lake 40 Challenge. The 1923 reports were striking, detailing disappearances and animal attacks that local folklore attributed to a forbidden ritual called "The Shadow Summoning." This ritual summoned spirits and grant the participant visions of the future, but it came with a heavy price—those who performed it often vanished without a trace, and wildlife in the area became aggressive.

Dom knew he was onto something significant. The Lake 40 Challenge wasn't just an urban legend—it had deep roots that stretched back decades, even centuries. The journal, the missing girl, the bear attacks—they were all pieces of a much larger, more sinister puzzle.

As the night had deepened around him, and the house was silent except for the occasional creak of settling wood. Dom glanced at the clock on his computer screen and realized how much time had passed. The sun would rise soon. His eyes burned from staring at the screen, and his body ached with exhaustion.

He jotted down the contact information for the historian who ran the local history website and would reach out to them in the morning.

When he couldn't stay awake any longer. The information he had uncovered was overwhelming, and his mind buzzed with new questions and the chilling realization that they were facing something far beyond the ordinary. The veil between the living and the dead was thin here, and something dark was seeping through.

After shutting down his computer, he staggered to bed. As he lay down, the details of the old reports and the day's discoveries swirled in his mind. He knew that sleep would bring no peace, but his body demanded rest. The case had awakened a part of him he had long kept hidden. Now, it seemed, there was no turning back.

CHAPTER 4

June 5, 2019

The soft glow of my laptop is the only light in the room. My journal lies open, filled with scribbled notes and thoughts. The last thing I tried was the Fade ritual. At first, it was super disappointing when nothing seemed to happen. But then there was the lost time. Since then, it feels like I haven't been alone. Something is watching me. The sensation is intense, like eyes boring into the back of my head.

Being alone in the apartment now doesn't help. Both of my roommates are gone for sure—Casey is abroad in Hong Kong for the summer, and Jenna has moved in with her boyfriend, though she occasionally comes back to grab more stuff. It's strange having the place to myself all the time now. The silence is overwhelming, amplifying every creak and groan of the old apartment. Our walls seem bare and foreboding. The air is still, and I can feel the absence of my roommates. Tonight, knowing I'm alone but feeling a presence puts me on edge.

I wander through the apartment, each step echoing in the empty rooms. The kitchen, once bustling with cooking and chatting, is now silent. The only sound is the faint hum of the refrigerator. I pause in the living room, the old wooden floors creaking underfoot. The shadows seem to dance along the walls, and I swear I see them shift and twist out of the corner of my eye. Every small noise is amplified, making me jump.

Earlier at work, something creepy happened. I was stocking shelves in the dairy aisle when I felt a cold draft, even though there shouldn't have been any. The air conditioning doesn't reach that part of the store. Then, out of nowhere, all the milk cartons on the top shelf tipped over at once, like they'd been pushed by an invisible hand. My heart nearly stopped. The store was empty, and no one else was around. I tried to laugh it off, but the unease hasn't gone away.

I shake my head, trying to dispel the creeping dread. My pen on the crisp paper grounds me. Isn't this what I wanted? To experience things? To feel the thrill of the unknown? As I write, my mind drifts back to the dream. I see myself standing in a dark, moonlit landscape, the air thick with anticipation. Luke is there, waiting for me by the Statue of Liberty. We agreed to meet here, in this dreamscape, but something feels wrong. The statue's eyes follow us, and the surrounding shadows seem to move with a life of their own. Luke's voice is distant, echoing as if from far away. We talk, but the words are a blur, overshadowed by the oppressive atmosphere. When I messaged him later, asking if he was in my dream, he didn't answer clearly. Instead, he replied, "Dreams are strange, aren't they? Sometimes it's hard to tell what's real and what isn't."

The first time I tried a ritual, I was twelve. It was a simple one, something I found in a dusty old book at the library. I remember the thrill of lighting the candles, the scent of wax mingling with the old paper smell of the book. Nothing happened then, either, but I was hooked. The possibility, the what-if, was enough to keep me coming back. Now, years later, that same thrill courses through me, mixed with a gnawing fear that I might be in over my head.

I snap back to the present, a shiver running down my spine. Understanding what happened becomes an urgent need, so I spend hours on forums, reading about others experiences and looking for patterns. The feeling of being watched is constant now; mirrors reflect things that shouldn't be there, shadows seem deeper, and the air feels heavy with unseen eyes. One user, ShadowSeeker91, wrote, "After doing 'The Fade,' I kept seeing reflections of myself doing things I wasn't doing. Like, I'd be brushing my hair in the mirror, but in reality, I was just standing there. Freaked me out." Another post by WhisperingWraith mentioned, "Sometimes I feel like someone is behind me, just out of sight. Every time I turn around, there's nothing there. But the feeling never goes away." These stories fuel my curiosity and fear in equal measure.

Determined to find answers, I decide to review my journal from the night of the lost time. Flipping through, I come across a slip of paper tucked into the pages I don't remember writing. The handwriting is mine, but the words are unfamiliar.

The shadows are whispering. They know my name.

A chill runs down my spine. I check my body for any marks and find a strange bruise on my forearm, shaped like a faint symbol. How did it get there? The unease intensifies, but I can't stop now.

The only way to know is to do it again. Practice makes perfect, right? At least Mom might appreciate that I'm trying to excel at whatever I do. With determination, I set up the mirrors and candle once more. This familiar setup feels different, more ominous. The gilded mirror from the common room gleams, its intricate frame casting strange shadows. Meanwhile, the plain rectangle from my bathroom reflects a distorted version of me, and the small hand mirror adds an unsettling third eye to the triangle.

As I chant the incantation, the air grows colder. The flame flickers as if caught in a breeze that doesn't exist. This time, I hear faint whispers, see fleeting shapes in the mirrors, and feel a presence growing closer. My heart races, the room pressing in on me. There is a shadow in the mirror behind me. Is it my own?

The ritual ends, leaving me breathless and confused. Unsure if anything happened, I listen as the whispers fade, but the sense of being watched intensifies. On the brink of discovering something vast and unknown, I sit in my room, surrounded by notes and journals, realizing how deep I've gone but unable to pull back. A whisper of my name in the darkness sends a chill through me. Turning, I see nothing—or do I? The shadow on the wall moves, and a fleeting touch on my shoulder confirms it. I'm not alone, and I'm too far gone to turn back now.

I decide I need to talk to someone about this. My phone buzzes, and I see a message from Taylor. She's one of the few people who knows about my interest in the paranormal, even if she doesn't share it.

Taylor: "Hey, how's your summer going?"

I hesitate for a moment before replying.

Me: "Weird, honestly. Can we talk? I had another strange experience."

Taylor: "Sure, want to meet up for coffee?"

Me: "Yeah, that'd be great. Same place?"

Taylor: "Yep, see you in 30."

As I prepare to leave, I notice the shadows seem less oppressive. Maybe talking to Taylor will help clear my mind.

I grab my journal, hoping that by sharing my experiences,
I might find some clarity.

Chapter 5

October 16, 2019

Dom dragged himself into the station around nine, eyes gritty from lack of sleep. With only a couple of hours of rest, his mind wouldn't stop spinning on the case. Now at his cluttered desk, he finished a cup of coffee while flipping through his notes. The stark fluorescent lights overhead did nothing to ease the pounding in his head. In front of him lay the journal, dry and warped. The designs on the cover seemed to mock him, daring him to delve deeper into its mysteries.

He had spoken with Mrs. Chen when he first arrived. They agreed to meet after five when she and her husband got home from work. She seemed hopeful that someone was working on the case. This was one of the harder aspects of missing persons. He could almost taste her gratitude that someone was on Lily's case, but he knew how these things ended and didn't want to give her false hope.

Lauren walked in shortly after and made a beeline for the coffee machine. She poured herself a cup and then another one for Dom, the smell of the fresh brew cutting through the thick fog of exhaustion.

She handed Dom the cup without a word, sitting across from him. They shared a quiet moment, sipping their coffee. It was Dom who broke the silence first.

"You alright?" he asked.

Lauren stared into her mug, her shoulders tense. "I'm fine—just tired."

Dom glanced at her, seeing the dark circles under her eyes. Lauren rarely talked about what was going on with her and Natalie, but it was clear something was weighing on her mind.

"You can't hold it in forever," Dom said, meeting her eyes. "You need someone in your corner. Might as well be me."

Lauren sighed, her voice shaky. "She said some things that... hit hard. She accused me of being distant, of hiding behind work. Maybe she's right, in a way, but..."

"She's not the only one who hides behind something," Dom said.

Lauren's frustration was evident. "I try to be there for her, but it's like no matter what I do, it's never enough. I can't seem to reach her, and she refuses to get help."

Dom took a sip of his coffee. "You can't force her," he said. "Maybe... you're the one that needs to give in and get the help."

Lauren pressed her lips together into a thin line. "I'll think about it."

Dom drained the last of his coffee. "Let's get to work," he said, his voice steady. "We've got a lot to do."

Lauren followed suit, determination replacing the fatigue in her eyes. "Right," she agreed.

The missing person's case was strange. Lily Chen had first been reported missing to the Everett Police Department. Like many cities in the U.S., it faced a rampant opioid crisis and significant homelessness. When a young adult living near downtown was reported missing, overdose was often the first suspicion, and this case seemed no different.

But Lily Chen was an exception. She came from an affluent family. Everett borders some of the wealthiest areas in Washington State. Both of Lily's parents were professionals—her mother a doctor and her father an engineer at Boeing. This detail shifted the case from the routine "we will find a body soon" pile to the jurisdiction of the Snohomish County Major Crimes Unit. Since August, it had been their responsibility to solve the mystery of Lily's disappearance.

The only substantial piece of evidence tying Lily to the Lake 40 trail was a statement by her friend, Taylor

Mitchell, age 21. Taylor had dropped Lily off for a hike around the time she vanished. She described Lily as excited yet reserved about the hike. Taylor mentioned Lily had been talking about some "challenge" she had read about online, involving obscure rituals and a place called Lake 40. This seemed to line up with the journal they had found at the more recent scene.

Dom couldn't shake the feeling that they were dealing with something far beyond a standard missing person case. The lines between legend and reality, sanity and madness, were difficult to discern.

The drive to the Chen family's home was somber. An autumn sun cast long shadows across the streets, painting the suburban landscape in hues of gold and orange. Dom's thoughts were a turbulent mix of case details and the eerie sense of the supernatural that had seemed to creep into their investigation.

Lauren broke the silence. "Do you think this is connected to that Lake 40 Challenge? It sounds like an urban legend, but there's something about this that feels... different."

Dom kept his eyes on the road, his grip on the steering wheel tightening. "I don't know. There's something off about this whole thing, and we need to spread out all the pieces before attempting to put them together."

A hearty laugh escaped Lauren. This was the first time he had seen her smile today.

"You and your snippets of wisdom," she said between giggles.

They pulled up to the Chen residence, a stately home in the quiet, upscale neighborhood of Mill Creek. As they approached the front door, Dom steeled himself for the difficult conversation ahead. He hoped this visit would shed more light on Lily's mysterious disappearance.

Dr. Chen opened the door, her eyes red-rimmed and weary. She forced a polite smile. "Detectives, please come in."

She gestured toward a table in the nearby dining room. As Dom followed her, Lauren gave him a light smack on the arm, then glanced from his feet to the mat by the door. His face reddened as he took off his shoes.

Mr. Chen was already standing by the table. He greeted Dom and Lauren before pulling out a chair for his wife. The dining room exuded an air of refined elegance with its polished mahogany table. Dr. Chen sat down, her posture erect and composed despite the obvious strain in her eyes. Lauren and Dom settled into the plush, high-backed chairs across from the Chens, their presence seeming almost out of place in such a pristine setting.

"Dr. and Mr. Chen, I am Detective Dom Dupont, and this is my partner, Detective Lauren Kim. We have some potential leads on Lily's case and wanted to meet with you in light of recent evidence."

"Of course, Detective," Mr. Chen said. His voice was quiet and measured, but the stress in his eyes was evident.

"I'm so sorry for what you both must be going through," Lauren said. "We just need to go through the statements you already made to catch Detective Dupont and me up to speed."

"What additional evidence have you found?" Dr. Chen asked, her voice tinged with a mixture of hope and apprehension.

"We will get to that after we review a few things," Dom replied, trying to be gentle.

Dr. Chen gave a quick nod.

"According to the information we have, Lily lived with two other roommates in Everett, Washington. She attended Everett Community College and was working toward a transfer degree. She worked at the food co-op on Colby and did not have a car or drive. You paid her rent, and there was no financial hardship that you know of. Is all of this correct so far?" Dom asked.

"That's right," Mr. Chen replied.

"In the file, it is mentioned that you do not know who her closest friends are. Did she ever invite anyone to your home, or did she have a boyfriend or girlfriend you know of?" Lauren asked.

"No," Dr. Chen answered this time. "Lily focused on her studies; she did not have time for friends. Her roommates are Casey Li and Jenna Thompson. Both are obedient young adults and students."

"Dear," Mr. Chen interjected, "we need to be open if they are going to help."

He turned to Dom. "Lily is an excellent student, but she had a fascination with the supernatural that distracted her sometimes. My father, her grandfather, was the same way. They bonded over it. We did not approve, so she stopped sharing that part of her life with us."

Dr. Chen's lips were set in a thin line. "It was mostly a phase," she said with a sniff.

"Did you know the young woman who reported her missing?" Dom asked. "Taylor Mitchell?"

"We had never met her," Mr. Chen replied.

Dom jotted down notes. "Are there any recent updates or changes you've noticed? Anything out of the ordinary since our last visit?"

Mr. Chen hesitated for a moment before speaking. "We went to her apartment recently to collect some of her belongings. We found her laptop, but we do not know the password."

He handed the laptop to Dom. "We thought it might be helpful."

Dom accepted the laptop. "Thank you, Mr. Chen. This could indeed be useful. We'll treat it as evidence and see what we can find."

"Wait, what additional evidence did you find?" Dr. Chen asked, a mix of hope and concern in her voice.

Lauren answered, "we recently came across a journal that might shed some light on the case. It's providing us with some new leads."

"Can we have it?"

Dom shook his head. "I'm sorry, Dr. Chen, but it's evidence."

Lauren added, "We'll keep you updated with any developments. Please contact us if you remember anything else or notice anything unusual."

Both detectives were quiet as they pulled away from the Chen household.

"Typical," Lauren scoffed. "High expectations, stressed kid. I wouldn't be surprised if—"

"She is not you, Lauren," Dom interrupted. "But I can see why you connect with her." He glanced over at his partner in time to catch her scowl. "How about dinner? There's a great Mexican place nearby."

"Sorry," Lauren sighed. "I need to get home. Trying to do better for Natalie. She needs me, lets just head to Lily's apartment, then wrap up."

It would be another night alone, with takeout for him.

"You need to get a woman," Lauren snickered.

Dom just shook his head. He wouldn't do that to anyone. He had his own issues to figure out before attempting any sort of relationship.

The autumn night had settled in by the time Dom and Lauren arrived at Lily's apartment. The building was quiet, the only sound the rustling of leaves in the cool breeze. Dom glanced at the keys the Chens had given him, a reminder of the responsibility they carried.

The apartment was on the third floor, and the climb up the stairs felt more daunting than usual. Dom unlocked the door and pushed it open, revealing a space frozen in time. It was as if Lily had just stepped out for a moment and would return any second. Her textbooks were scattered on the coffee table, a half-empty mug of tea sat on the counter, and a pile of laundry lay folded on the couch.

Lauren flicked on the lights, casting a warm glow over the room. "Let's start with her bedroom," she suggested, heading down the short hallway.

Dom followed, feeling a strange sense of intrusion. Lily's room was tidy, with posters of various bands and scenic landscapes adorning the walls. Her bed was made, and another journal rested on the nightstand. Dom picked it up, flipping through the pages filled with notes and sketches.

As he skimmed, a sudden chill ran down his spine. He glanced around the room, feeling an unshakable presence. He tried to hide his reaction, but Lauren noticed something was off.

"Dom, what's wrong?" she asked, her voice concerned.

He shook his head, trying to brush it off. "Nothing, just a weird feeling."

Lauren narrowed her eyes, but didn't press further. "Let's keep looking. There might be something here that could help us."

They spent the next hour searching the apartment and going through Lily's belongings. Dom couldn't shake the eerie sensation that they weren't alone, and it was clear Lauren was picking up on it, too. She glanced at him occasionally.

"Dom, if there's something bothering you, you need to tell me," she said, breaking the silence.

Dom sighed, leaning against the kitchen counter. "I just... I feel like there's a presence here. Like Lily never really left."

Lauren's expression softened. "You think her spirit is still here?"

"I don't know. Maybe. It just feels... off," Dom admitted, running a hand through his hair.

"Lets just stay focused so we can go home."

Dom appreciated her support. "You're right. Let's finish up here and get some rest. We have a lot to go through tomorrow."

They wrapped up their search, taking a few more items of interest, including the journal Dom had found. As they locked up and headed back to the car.

Once they were back at the station, Lauren took off. Dom headed to the IT office, the laptop from Lily's apartment tucked under his arm. The night shift was in full swing. The door was ajar, and Dom pushed it open to find Detective Ray Collins, the department's lead forensic specialist, typing away at his computer. Collins looked up as Dom entered, his eyes lighting up with interest at the sight of the laptop.

"Got something for me, Dupont?" Collins asked, leaning back in his chair.

"Yeah, Ray," Dom said, setting the laptop on the desk. "This is Lily Chen's laptop. Her parents found it at her apartment but didn't know the password. We need to see if there's anything on it that might give us a lead."

Collins reached for a notepad to jot down the details. "Alright, I'll get to work on it first thing in the morning. The guys have already gone home for the night, and I'll need their help to get through it."

Dom felt a twinge of impatience but kept his tone measured. "Any chance you can give me an estimate on how long it might take? I'd like to know what's on it as soon as possible."

Collins shrugged, glancing at the laptop. "If it's just a standard password crack, we could have it done within a few hours. But if she's encrypted the data or if there's a lot to sift through, it might take longer. I'll give you an update as soon as we make progress."

Dom appreciated the straightforward response. "Alright, I'll check back with you in the morning. Just... this could be a big break in the case. Appreciate you jumping on it."

Collins gave a reassuring smile. "You got it, Dom. We'll do our best."

Dom left the IT office, the sense of urgency still gnawing at him. As much as he wanted to stay and wait, he knew it would be more practical to get some rest and come back fresh in the morning. He walked back through the station and headed home for another solitary night with takeout.

Chapter 6

June 8, 2019

The more I delve into the Fade game, the more it hooks me. The missing time aspect is gripping, pulling me into an obsession with everything related to the Fade. Examples of it are scattered throughout literature and media, mostly sinister. Yet, every story has some aspect of truth, right? Not everything has to be the Upside Down. Tír na nÓg is a good place, and Avalon? I suspect those worlds intersect. My grandfather tells me stories about Penglai, the island of immortals. That sounds good too. Places where reality thins and other realms seep through.

Summer session has started. I'm taking Calculus and an Intro to Astronomy course (I need an elective). In the fall, I'll transfer to UW. I also picked up extra shifts at the store since my course load is lighter. It seemed like a good idea, but now it's interfering with my research on the Fade.

I start with "places like the Fade" and end up with more fictional stuff. But the Crossroads grab me. It seems similar to what I'm experiencing. However, the search is full of demonic lore. I find a thread about having a conversation with Legba, but it feels disrespectful to someone else's religion. I'm approaching this from a secular place.

After a while, I stumble upon another one of those urban legend 'games.' It's close to the Fade game. I'm thinking of giving this a shot tomorrow night. It involves another candle, a dark room, and whispered chants. What's the worst that could happen, right? There's a strange thrill in not knowing.

I keep searching in case something better comes up. There seem to be lots of games to play with your friends, but few for solo adventurers. What are you supposed to do if you don't have friends or if they don't share your creepy intrigue? Most of them are designed for a good scare—Bloody Mary, the Candyman. Even the Ouija board is like that. Those just seem stupid. Why would I want to summon a Candyman whose goal is to kill me? I'm much more interested in stuff like the Elevator Game, where I could explore an alternate reality. But without a car and no ten-story buildings within walking distance, I need to dig deeper.

There are a few I jot down for later, but the candle one seems best: The Picture Game: Involves a group of people but can be adapted for solo play. You need a camera and several items to create a circle. Participants take turns snapping photos within the circle to capture ghostly images. The Doors of Your Mind: This is a mental game where you explore a series of doors in your mind, each leading to different rooms or scenarios. The game involves meditation and visualization techniques.

I wonder if I enter some sort of version of the Fade when I practice my lucid dreaming. This makes me think of Luke. I open up Discord to send a message.

DreamSeeker: You there?

I wait a few minutes but get no reply. He's somewhere in Florida, and it's 10 p.m. here. Most likely, he's asleep.

DreamSeeker: If you get this, I'll be at General Sherman.

We have both been to Sequoia National Park, so it seems a good option to try. I don't expect him to be there. But even if he isn't, trees are ancient and there is probably some amazing residual energy.

Laying in bed, I don't remember falling asleep, but before I know it, I'm floating above my body. I catch some movement out of the corner of my eye, but when I turn to look, it's gone. I have read the warnings to be careful when you leave your body—something evil might jump in and you could be trapped in your dreams. But who would be interested in stealing my body?

I think about General Sherman, and suddenly, I'm there. In my dreams, I live in a sort of perpetual transitional time between dawn and day. It's gray, just light enough to see the world around me, but fuzzy. I sit against the tree, soaking it all in, when I hear a voice call my name. It's soft and masculine.

"Luke?" I call out.

I stand up and look around the tree, but don't see anyone. Then I walk a little down the trail in the direction the voice came from. My name is called again from behind me—soft like a whisper. I turn around fast this time, just in time to see a flash of something disappear behind one of the other redwood trees. I follow it, but when I get around the giant tree, I don't see him. What is Luke playing at?

Then I hear it again and again, strange whispers all around me.

"Wake up!" the voice says.

A chill runs down my spine as the whispers grow more urgent, overlapping, surrounding me in a cacophony of soft, insistent voices. The world around me seems to pulse, the trees swaying in a wind that isn't there. Shadows deepen, and the gray light dims further, as if the forest itself is closing in.

"Wake up!" they chant in unison, louder and louder.

Panic surges within me. I spin around, trying to locate the source, but the forest is empty save for the towering redwoods. My heart pounds, and the air grows thick, almost tangible, pressing against my skin. I have to get out, but I don't know how. The whispers become deafening, a roaring tide of voices that drowns out all thought.

The ground beneath me seems to shift, and I feel myself falling, the forest spinning into darkness.

I jolt awake, drenched in sweat, my room silent. The memory of the whispers lingers, and I can't shake the feeling that something has followed me back. The line between the Fade and reality has never felt thinner.

Chapter 7

October 17, 2019

Dom sat at his desk in the station, the hum of activity around him barely registering as he stared at the journal in front of him. The fluorescent lights above cast a harsh glow, but all he could see was the dim light of his bathroom from the night before, the shadows stretching and twisting like they were alive.

He couldn't seem to stay away from the rabbit hole of the paranormal. When he was younger, he had scoffed at his Mémère's wisdom. But now, he wished he could call her. He had taken the journal home with him last night without checking it out as evidence. Lauren was going to be on his case for working off hours and not checking out evidence. Something about that Fade ritual seemed off to him. Well, not just the Fade ritual—all of it.

Mémère would have told him to leave it be. This was work for a manbo, not the likes of him. He would have listened, too—he had no interest in all that. But he didn't have her to turn to. All he had was the journal and a hunch. It wasn't even a hunch he could share.

Dom's mind drifted back to the previous night. In his bathroom, the air had felt heavy and suffocating, as if the walls were closing in on him. Attempting the Fade ritual that Lily had practiced so many times, he used the bathroom mirror, an old hand mirror, and a shiny pan that was reflective enough for the purpose. The mismatched mirrors created a distorted, disorienting effect, each reflection warping into the next.

As he walked through the steps, exhaustion had hit him like a wave. The room had grown colder, and the air was thick. He hadn't felt himself drifting until his head crashed against the bathroom mirror, waking him up. For a split second before he woke, he swore he saw a young Asian woman pounding on his mirror. But she was on the other side.

Dom's heart had pounded in his chest as he stared at his reflection, his breath fogging the glass. The woman's image was gone, but the chill remained. He had backed away from the mirror, his legs shaky, the sense of unease growing. The shadows in the room had seemed to deepen, the corners of the bathroom becoming dark voids.

The silence had been oppressive, broken only by the faint hum of the refrigerator in the next room. Dom had tried to shake off the vision, telling himself it was just a trick of the light, his mind playing tricks on him, or even a dream. But the feeling of being watched had persisted. He could almost hear the faint whispers just beyond the edge of hearing, like voices from another world trying to break through.

Mémère had always warned him about tampering with the unknown, about the dangers that lurked just beyond the veil. "There are places you shouldn't go, things you shouldn't see," she had told him. "Leave it to those who know the ways, who can protect themselves."

But he couldn't leave it alone. The journal was a key, a connection to something beyond the mundane world. He had to understand what had happened to Lily, what she had seen. He had to know if there was any truth to the rituals, any reality to the whispers of another world.

As Dom delved deeper, he couldn't help but connect it to his parents' deaths and the strange, fragmented memories that haunted him. Shadows of half-remembered scenes from his childhood resurfaced. He recalled his mother's fearful eyes and his father's hushed conversations about things they couldn't explain. The journal, with its eerie entries, seemed to unlock parts of his past he could never quite access. The need to uncover the truth became a relentless drive, intertwining Lily's fate with his own search for answers.

He had sat down on the bathroom floor, his back against the cool tile, and opened the journal again. The pages had seemed to pulse with energy, the words twisting and shifting as if they were alive. He read through Lily's entries, feeling her experiences, her growing obsession with the Fade.

Dom knew he was in over his head, but he didn't care. But he couldn't stop. He had to know the truth, had to understand what Lily had discovered.

After he had stood up, his legs were shaky. He looked at his reflection in the mirror. For a moment, he thought he saw the young woman again, her eyes filled with fear, her hands pressed against the glass as if trying to break through. But then she was gone, leaving only his own haunted reflection.

Back at the station, Dom shook himself out of his reverie. The memory of the previous night clung to him, the sense of dread and the vision of the woman. He glanced around, ensuring no one had noticed his distraction, and focused on the task at hand. The rabbit hole had opened, and there was no turning back.

He heard Ray Collins' voice behind him and he felt the hearty slap on his back.

"Dom Dupont," Detective Collins said. "I've got your laptop cracked."

Dom looked up from his desk, pushing aside the journal he had been lost in. He tried to shake off the unease.

"Thanks, Ray," Dom said, his voice steady.

The detective placed Lily's laptop on Dom's desk and slid a clipboard over for him to initial. "Just log it back into evidence when you're done."

As Dom opened the laptop and watched it boot up, Lauren sauntered in with two mochas.

"Starbucks day, is it?" Dom raised an eyebrow.

Lauren sat down next to him. "Whatcha got?"

"Laptop's cracked," Dom answered. He wondered how much of last night he should tell her, but judging by the coffee and her haggard face, he didn't want to burden her further. They would do this right.

Dom took a deep breath. He clicked through the folders on Lily's desktop, Lauren peering over his shoulder.

"Alright, let's see what we've got," he murmured.

The screen displayed a cluttered desktop with various icons. Dom navigated to the documents folder first.

"Here we go, school stuff," he said, opening a folder labeled 'EVCC.'

Lauren sipped her mocha, her eyes scanning the screen. "Class schedules, assignments... typical student files."

Dom clicked on a document titled 'Summer 2019 Schedule.' "Let's start here." He scrolled through the file. "Intro to Astronomy, Calculus, and... Lab partner: Ava Martinez."

"Ava, okay. We should track her down and see if she knows anything," Lauren noted.

"Agreed," Dom said, making a mental note. He continued to sift through the files, opening various assignments and project notes. Nothing seemed out of the ordinary.

"Let's check her emails," Lauren suggested.

Dom navigated to the email client and opened it. They skimmed through a series of mundane messages: reminders from teachers, group project discussions, and work schedules from the food co-op. One email stood out—an exchange with her astronomy professor discussing an upcoming lab project.

"Looks like she was pretty involved in her classes," Dom commented.

"Nothing here screams red flags. Let's move on to her contacts."

Dom opened her Google Contacts, scrolling through the list of names. He paused when he saw Taylor Mitchell's contact information.

"Here's Taylor," he said. "Let's talk to her. She might have more insights."

"Yeah, definitely. We need to see if she's noticed anything unusual or if Lily mentioned anything about the rituals."

Dom clicked through a few more contacts, making notes of any names that seemed relevant, but nothing else stood out.

"Alright, let's dig into her messages and Discord," Dom suggested.

They opened the messaging app and started scrolling through her recent chats. Most were mundane conversations with classmates and work colleagues, discussing assignments, weekend plans, and the occasional meme or joke. But it was when they clicked on one server that things took a more intriguing turn.

Most of her DMs were between her and a user named 'ArdentElan'. The bulk of their conversations seemed to take place on a server that this person ran, filled with channels about various supernatural topics.

"Here we go," Dom said, leaning closer to the screen. "Look at this. It's a goldmine of supernatural discussions."

Lauren's eyes widened. "Most of her activity is here. Look at the intensity of their conversations."

They scrolled through, noting detailed discussions about rituals, the Fade, and other paranormal phenomena. Lily and Luke exchanged theories, experiences, and plans for future rituals.

"This guy is deeply into the same stuff as Lily," Lauren said, a hint of unease in her voice.

"Yeah, too into it," Dom agreed. "But it looks like this server could have more clues. We need to go through it carefully."

Dom clicked on Lily's DMs with Luke. The conversations were extensive, filled with messages about their latest findings, ritual instructions, and personal thoughts. They read through the last few messages, noting that the last conversation was dated July 31st.

"This was the last time they talked," Dom said, frowning.

Lauren leaned closer. "That's right before she went missing. You don't think... We need to find this guy."

"I'll get the tech team to trace his account, see if we can find out who he really is. We'll need a warrant for that, though."

"I'll get the paperwork started." Lauren looked at him as she stood up. "Dom, do you think there's more to this than just some online obsession?"

Dom met her gaze, the memory of the previous night flashing in his mind. "I don't know, Lauren. But whatever it is, we're going to understand it."

As soon as Lauren walked away, Dom turned back to the computer. He knew better, but couldn't resist. The urge to uncover the truth about Lily's disappearance was too strong to ignore. He navigated to the settings in Discord and changed Lily's account password. He made a mental note of the new password, ensuring he could access it later if needed.

Dom then pulled out his phone and logged into Lily's Discord account using the new credentials. His hands shook as he typed, the tension from the previous night still gripping him. The app loaded, and he saw the familiar chat interface.

"Are you there?" he typed from Lily's account.

He waited, his heart pounding in his chest. The seconds seemed to stretch into minutes, each moment filled with a heavy silence. There was no reply. The chat window remained still, mocking him with its emptiness. Dom felt a mixture of frustration and guilt. He knew he had crossed a line, but the desperation to find out what had happened to Lily overpowered his sense of propriety.

Just as he heard Lauren returning, he deleted the message and closed the chat window. He took a deep breath, trying to steady himself and hide any trace of his clandestine activity. The guilt nagged at him, but he pushed it aside, focusing on the urgency of the case.

Lauren set her coffee down and sat back beside him, her expression determined but tired. "Filed," she stated.

"Thanks. It will be a few days for that to come through, but there's a lot to go on here. Let's focus on what we can use."

They turned their attention back to the laptop. Dom's mind wandered, pulled back to memories of his Mémère, and the tales she would tell him. He remembered her small, cluttered kitchen in New Orleans, the air always thick with the scent of incense and herbs. She had warned him about the dangers of the unseen world, her voice a mixture of wisdom and caution.

"You have the gift, Dom," she would say, her eyes serious and full of love. "But with it comes responsibility. There are things out there that you must respect, and some you must fear."

He had scoffed at her then, dismissing her stories as old-world superstition. But as he grew older, especially after joining the force and encountering cases that defied logic, he realized how much truth there was in her words. Those lessons came rushing back now, the echoes of her warnings blending with the urgency of the current case.

Dom glanced at Lauren. She was jotting down notes; her focus was intense despite the fatigue that lined her face. He knew she was struggling at home, her relationship with Natalie fraying under the stress. She had confided in him more than once, the vulnerability in her eyes a stark contrast to her usual tough exterior.

"Lauren," he said, "how you holding up?"

She paused, looking up from her notes, and managed a weary smile. "I'm fine, Dom. Just... tired. But we've got work to do."

"Yeah, we do. Let's make a plan."

"I'll call Ava and Taylor right away. See if they can meet with us today." Lauren replied.

Dom leaned back, rubbing his temples. "I'll message Ray and get the ball rolling on tracing ArdentElan's account. We'll need that warrant as soon as possible."

They worked in silence for a while, the station's background noise fading as they focused on their tasks.

After a few minutes, Lauren hung up her phone and looked over at him. "Ava can meet us this afternoon. Taylor is harder to pin down, but she said she'd call back with a time."

"Good," Dom said. "The more information we can gather, the better."

"Dom," Lauren broke the silence, her voice softer. "Do you ever feel... lonely?"

Dom looked up, meeting her eyes. He saw the vulnerability there, the fear she tried to hide. "All the time," he admitted.

"It's been hard, with Natalie. She doesn't understand, and I can't blame her. But this job... it gets under your skin."

Dom reached out, giving her hand a reassuring squeeze. She smiled.

They gathered their notes and prepared to leave the station. As they walked out into the crisp air, the surrounding city buzzed with life. For Dom and Lauren, the world had narrowed to their mission.

Just as they were about to step into Lauren's car, Dom's phone buzzed. He pulled it out, seeing a new notification. It was from Lily's Discord account. His pulse quickened as he opened it.

The message was brief, sent from the user 'ArdentElan':

"I know what you're looking for. Stop before it's too late."

Dom stared at the screen, his heart racing.

"What is it?" Lauren asked.

"Nothing," Dom lied, locking his phone. "Just an ad."

CHAPTER 8

June 14, 2019

I haven't been sleeping well. Today, I wake to Taylor's light snore on the couch. She came by last night at my request. Although she has her own house, she never talks about how she got it, and I don't ask. She always comes here and never invites me over, which is strange.

I met Taylor during my first year at EVCC. We were in a composition class together. It's hard to believe, since I journal and all, but I hate writing. Taylor is brilliant. She's what got me through that class. She writes amazing short stories and poetry that evoke so many feelings. And it's dark too—which is strange because she is such a bright person.

Next to her, I feel boring—the quiet math girl. Her home life is a mystery to me. There are rumors about her father's death, possibly murder, maybe suicide, but I try not to push and ignore the gossip. She is my friend, and I trust she will tell me when and if she needs to.

She didn't want to sleep in one of my roommates' beds—thought it was weird, so now I tiptoe to make some coffee. I don't have any classes today, but I need to meet with my advisor. The quarter just started, and I've already missed two classes. I know she's going to recommend dropping and taking the classes in the fall. But I really want to finish the transfer degree so I can start at UW.

I don't want to admit it, but I may have to lay off the supernatural stuff a bit. That Fade game still has my head spinning, though. Maybe I'll try it one more time after going over my notes with Luke. Obviously, it didn't fail—with the lost time and all. But I want to remember. Perhaps moving in the Fade is like lucid dreaming—I just need techniques to control it better.

My skin crawls. The last time I tried the lucid dream, it terrified me. The strange whispers—just all-around creepy. I have not connected with Luke to know if he had been there. Maybe this stuff was all bullshit, and my parents were right. Maybe it was just giving me bad dreams and poor sleep.

"Mmphh..." Taylor mumbles and sits up.

"Sorry," I say. "Just making coffee and heading to school."

"You look like your head is going to explode," Taylor giggles. "What's going on?"

"Nothing," I shrug. "Just thinking that I need take a break from the paranormal shit for a while."

Taylor stands, looking much more awake. "No! Don't do that. It's what keeps you sane!"

I love her. Even if it's not her thing, she is so supportive. No one (aside from Luke) has ever supported this part of me. I was never a BFF type of gal, but if anyone was, it would be Taylor.

"You got this!" she says. "Tell you what—before I go, I'll go down a Google rabbit hole about the Fade, and jot you down some notes—okay?"

I smile. "Thanks, T. I appreciate you."

"Anything for you. I'll see you soon!"

Later, when I get home, I see a torn-out piece of notebook paper on the counter. It has a list of websites on it, with the last one circled and a little side note saying, "This one is local!" I set the paper aside. My meeting with my advisor was what I had expected. I needed to do my calculus homework first—then paranormal research would be a reward.

After about an hour of equations, I hear a ping from Discord. I try to resist bringing up the window, but I have not heard from Luke in days, and I need to see if it's him.

ArdentElan: Sorry I missed General Sherman—been busy with work and school.

DreamSeeker: I could swear you were there. I heard your voice. Things got strange.

ArdentElan: Strange like how?

DreamSeeker: Like we were not alone.

ArdentElan: What do you mean? Did something else happen?

DreamSeeker: I heard whispers, saw shadows. It felt like something was watching us. Have you ever had a lucid dream go wrong?

ArdentElan: Once. I tried to control it too much, and it turned into a nightmare. The more I pushed, the worse it got. Ended up feeling trapped. Maybe that's what happened to you?

DreamSeeker: Maybe. But it felt so real, like it wasn't just a dream. Have you heard of the Fade causing this kind of interaction?

ArdentElan: Not specifically, but I've read that places where reality thins can lead to experiences that blur the line between dreams and waking life. It's possible you tapped into something deeper.

DreamSeeker: That's what I'm afraid of. I don't know how to navigate it.

ArdentElan: Maybe approach it like lucid dreaming. Stay calm, don't force control. Let it unfold naturally and observe. But also, don't ignore the risks. If it feels wrong, pull back.

DreamSeeker: Good advice. I'll try that. Thanks, Luke.

After the conversation, I glance at the list of websites Taylor left for me. Instead, I decide to do a deep dive into lucid dreaming techniques and how they can go wrong. I spend hours reading through various forums and articles, noting the similarities to my own experiences.

Lucid dreaming is an art that requires practice and control. Techniques include reality checks, where you question whether you are dreaming throughout the day, and maintaining a dream journal to improve dream recall. Some suggest using mnemonic induction methods, repeating phrases like "I will recognize when I'm dreaming" before falling asleep. Others advocate for the Wake Back to Bed (WBTB) method, where you wake up after a few hours of sleep and stay awake for a short period before going back to sleep to increase the chances of lucid dreaming.

But I also read about the darker side. Dreams can spiral into nightmares if you lose control. Some people report encountering shadowy figures, experiencing sleep paralysis, or feeling trapped in a dream they can't wake from. The boundary between dream and reality can blur, leading to confusion and fear.

As I read, I wonder: was it just a dream? Or have I brushed against another reality? The more I learn, the more I realize how little I understand. But one thing is clear—I can't stop now. I need to know the truth, no matter how unsettling it might be. This dream for sure ties into the Fade.

I lay down in bed, determined to try lucid dreaming again. I close my eyes and repeat a phrase to myself, "I will recognize when I'm dreaming." The room is quiet, the only sound the soft hum of the air conditioner. I focus on my breathing, drifting into a meditative state.

As I doze off, I feel a strange sensation, like I'm sinking into the mattress. My body feels heavy, and a sense of unease washes over me. I try to remind myself that I'm safe, that it's just a dream, but the feeling intensifies.

I open my eyes—or at least I think I do—and find myself in a shadowy version of my room. The edges are blurred, and the light is dim. I get out of bed and walk to the door, but when I open it, I'm not in my apartment anymore. I'm standing in a dark, endless hallway. The walls are covered in a faint glow, and I hear whispers echoing around me.

"Wake up," the voices murmur, overlapping and growing louder. I try to turn back, but the door has disappeared. Panic rises in my chest, and I run down the hallway, my footsteps echoing in the emptiness.

I see a figure at the end of the hall. It's tall and cloaked in shadows, its face obscured. It stands motionless, but the whispers grow more insistent. "Wake up!"

I stop, frozen in place, as the figure moves toward me. The surrounding air grows cold, and I feel a pressure on my chest, making it hard to breathe. The whispers turn into a deafening roar, and the hallway spins.

Just as the figure reaches out to touch me, I jolt awake, drenched in sweat, my heart pounding. The room is silent, but the memory of the whispers lingers. I can't shake the feeling that something has followed me back.

CHAPTER 9

October 17, 2019

As they drove to Everett Community College to meet Ava Martinez, Lily's lab partner in her astronomy class, Dom felt a pang of guilt for keeping the Discord message with ArdentElan from Lauren. He didn't want her to get into any trouble if things went south.

"Ever been here before?" Dom asked, breaking the silence.

Lauren shook her head. "Nope, first time for me. You?"

"A couple of times. It's a nice campus," Dom replied, trying to sound casual.

"Hopefully, Ava can give us some new leads."

"Yeah, let's hope so," Dom said, eyes glued to the road.

The small campus was bustling with students, and cars were pouring out of the single entrance. It must be between classes, Dom thought. Like most community colleges, the student body was a melting pot of diversity. The parking lot and walkways teemed with a kaleidoscope of individuals, each representing a different chapter of life.

Young teenagers, likely Running Start students, darted through the throngs, their backpacks bouncing as they moved with the boundless energy of youth. Their animated chatter and uninhibited laughter differed from the more deliberate pace of older students, some navigating their second careers. These were men and women juggling classes with their jobs and family responsibilities. Dom spotted veterans among them, their military patches and disciplined bearing unmistakable, striving to forge a fresh path in civilian life. There were also single parents, clear by the occasional stroller and diaper bag.

After finding a parking spot, they made their way to a small coffee shop on campus. The rich aroma of brewed coffee permeated the air, blending with the soft murmur of conversation. Students occupied the small tables, some engrossed in their laptops, others engaged in animated discussions.

Dom and Lauren ordered their coffees and settled into a quiet corner to wait for Ava. As Dom scanned the room, he couldn't shake the sensation of Lily's presence, her connection to this place, and the community that surrounded her.

A small blonde woman approached them, squinting as she got closer. "Detective Kim?" she asked.

"That's me," Lauren replied with a warm smile. "Have a seat. Want anything?"

"I'm good," Ava replied. Her voice was soft. Dom couldn't tell if she was nervous or just shy. He tried to make his large body shrink to seem less imposing.

"I'm Detective Dupont," he said. "But you can call me Dom."

"Thanks," Ava smiled and eased into a seat.

Dom leaned forward, trying to put her at ease. "Ava, we appreciate you meeting with us. We understand you were Lily's lab partner. Can you tell us about your friendship?"

Ava's fingers twisted a strand of her hair. "We had our astronomy class together. She was really focused on this project about the lunar cycle, but often, she seemed... distracted."

"Did she ever mention anything specific about what was bothering her?" Lauren asked, her pen poised over her notebook.

"She talked a lot about the Fade," Ava said, her eyes darting around the room as if she was afraid someone might overhear. "She was obsessed with it, and liked to look at it scientifically."

Dom exchanged a glance with Lauren before continuing. "Did she ever mention anyone named Luke? He might have gone by the username ArdentElan online."

Ava frowned, thinking hard. "Luke? No, she didn't mention him by name, but she was always chatting with someone online. She said he was helping her with her research."

"How about Taylor Mitchell?" Lauren asked, her tone gentle but probing. "We heard they were close."

Ava's expression darkened. "Taylor... yeah, they were friends. Taylor seemed really hot and cold about all the paranormal stuff. They debated about it a lot."

Dom pieced together the information. "Did Lily ever mention any specific plans or rituals she was going to try? Anything that might have seemed dangerous?"

Ava hesitated, her eyes meeting Dom's. "She talked about a hike up near Granite Falls. Some lake. She said it was a ritual site connected to the Fade. She was planning something big, but she didn't tell me all the details, only that she would get some moon pictures for our project."

Dom's mind raced. "Ava, you've been very helpful. One last question—did Lily ever mention why she was so drawn to these rituals? Was there something she was searching for?"

Ava took a deep breath, her eyes reflecting a mixture of fear and sadness. "Not really. She said she wanted to understand the truth. Just looking for... answers, but I don't know what for."

"When's the last time you saw Lily?" Lauren asked.

As Ava leaned back in her chair. "The last time I saw Lily was in class the day she was supposed to go on that hike. She seemed excited but also kind of... preoccupied. She called me before she left her house too, but just to tell me she would send over pictures the next day. I never got them or heard from her again."

Ava looked as though she was about to cry. Dom leaned closer and spoke in a soft voice. "We will do everything we can to get answers."

"I know. Thank you."

As Lauren handed Ava a business card, she said, "Here is my number. If you think of anything else or just need to talk, don't hesitate."

Dom's eyes drifted over Ava's shoulder, scanning the room out of habit. In the far corner, he noticed a woman with dark hair watching them. She had an anxious, almost suspicious look. When Dom met her gaze, she turned and bolted for the door.

"Excuse me for a moment," Dom said, rising and moving toward the exit. The woman had already disappeared into the crowd outside by the time he reached the door.

He returned to the table, his mind racing. "Ava, do you know a woman with dark hair, about this tall?" he asked, indicating with his hand. "She was watching us just now."

Ava's eyes widened with recognition. "That sounds like Taylor. She must have seen us and gotten spooked."

Dom exchanged a look with Lauren, his instincts on high alert. "Keep my number handy too, just in case," he said, handing Ava his card.

The encounter added another layer of complexity to the case. Between Taylor's sudden flight and her tough schedule, it seemed she was hiding something.

Dom wasted no time once back at the station. He logged into his computer, determined to dive deep into Taylor Mitchell's background. His fingers flew across the keyboard, pulling up databases and cross-referencing information. Lauren watched him, her own thoughts preoccupied with the day's revelations.

Dom's screen filled with various records—public databases, social media profiles, and news articles. The first pieces of the puzzle were mundane: Taylor Mitchell, age 21, a student at Everett Community College, no criminal record. But as he dug deeper, the story took a darker turn.

He found an obituary for Taylor's father, Malcolm Mitchell, dated three years prior. The cause of death was listed as suicide. Dom's brow furrowed as he clicked on the article. Malcolm Mitchell had been the leader of a religious organization called the Children of the Veil, a group with a notorious reputation for dabbling in the paranormal and occult rituals. The organization had disbanded after his death, amid swirling rumors and allegations of misconduct.

"Lauren, look at this," Dom said, turning his monitor so she could see. "Taylor's father led a group involved in the paranormal. He died by suicide a few years ago."

"Sounds like a cult..." Lauren leaned in, her eyes scanning the screen. "The Children of the Veil... I've heard of them. They were pretty secretive. This can't be a coincidence."

"Lily's parents didn't seem to know much about Taylor's friends. It makes me wonder—did Lily find Taylor because of their mutual interest in the paranormal? How did they meet?"

He continued to dig, finding snippets of information that painted a picture of Taylor's life. She had grown up immersed in her father's world. From a young age, Taylor had been exposed to the rituals and beliefs of the Children of the Veil. Her father's teachings were a blend of mysticism, paranormal lore, and a Ardent belief in the supernatural. After his death, Taylor's life seemed to spiral. She became more withdrawn and fixated on the paranormal, perhaps to stay connected to her father.

Dom discovered that Taylor had been active in online forums dedicated to paranormal research, often discussing her father's work and seeking others who shared her interests. Her relationship with Malcolm had been complex; he was both a mentor and a figure of immense pressure. The cult's disbandment had left her adrift, searching for meaning and validation in the world her father had introduced her to.

"Lauren, I think Taylor was more than just a friend to Lily. She might have been a guide, someone who introduced her to these rituals. And ArdentElan... he's involved too, but I can't quite piece together how."

Lauren sighed, her fingers drumming on the desk. "This is getting more complicated by the minute. We need to find Taylor and talk to her."

Dom agreed. "We'll track her down. In the meantime, I'm going to keep digging into Malcolm Mitchell and the Children of the Veil. There might be more clues there about what Lily and Taylor were getting involved in."

Lauren stood and stretched. "I'll check with the tech team and see if they've made any progress on the warrant. Maybe there's something there that will help us."

Dom watched her leave, then turned back to his screen, a sense of urgency driving him. He needed to uncover the truth before anyone else got hurt. As he continued his search, he found an old newspaper clipping about a raid on the Children of the Veil's compound. The article described a night of chaos and fear, with cult members trying to shield their leader. The authorities had discovered disturbing evidence of bizarre rituals and illegal activities. Malcolm Mitchell, the group's charismatic yet dangerous leader, had orchestrated it all, leading his followers into a twisted and perilous existence.

Dom leaned back in his chair, absorbing what he had uncovered. Taylor had grown up in this environment, and it had shaped her worldview and actions. Her connection to Lily was no accident; it was a meeting of two minds drawn to the same dark mysteries.

He needed some sort of expert insight into these cult practices. He searched the college's faculty directory and found a Professor Jameson, who specialized in both psychology and history. His published works showed a keen interest in fringe religious movements.

Without hesitation, Dom composed an email outlining the basics of their case and requesting a meeting to discuss the Children of the Veil. He hit send and leaned back, expecting a long wait for a reply. To his surprise, a response pinged into his inbox within minutes.

"Detective Dupont, I'd be happy to assist. The Children of the Veil have been a personal research interest of mine for years. Can you come to my office tomorrow at 10 AM? Best regards, Professor Jameson."

Dom felt a surge of relief. He replied, confirming the appointment.

Later that night, Dom went home. Sleep came fitfully, haunted by the weight of the case and the dark mysteries surrounding it.

In his dream, he was a child again, running through a dark forest. He couldn't remember what he was running from, only that he had to keep moving. The trees loomed overhead, their branches like skeletal fingers reaching out to grab him. Fear gripped his heart, a primal terror that he couldn't shake. He stumbled and fell, the ground cold and unyielding beneath him. As he struggled to his feet, he heard whispers all around, voices calling his name, urging him to keep running. He had to escape, but from what, he couldn't remember.

He awoke in a cold sweat, the remnants of the nightmare clinging to his mind. The forest, the whispers, the fear—they had haunted him for as long as he could remember. He couldn't shake the feeling that his dream was a warning, a glimpse into the darkness that lay ahead.

After the nightmare, Dom couldn't sleep. He also could not get the Children of the Veil out of his head. His Mémère would just tut and go on about people messing with things they did not understand. Then, in the same breath, try to convince him to practice her faith with her. He sat at his desk, the pile of unread mail pushed aside, and opened his laptop. His stomach growled, but he had no appetite. The constant brain spin made food seem irrelevant. He typed "The Children of the Veil" and "Everett, Washington" into the search bar.

As he waited for the search results, his mind wandered back to the conversations he'd had with his Mémère. Her belief in the old ways often clashed with his modern sensibilities, yet now he found himself drawn into a world where such beliefs might hold some truth. The search results appeared, and Dom clicked on the first link that caught his eye:

Everett Tribune

Police Raid on "The Children of the Veil" Cult Uncovers Disturbing Practices

By Jess Staley, Investigative Reporter

Date: March 12, 2008

Everett, WA—In a dramatic turn of events, local authorities raided the compound of the religious group known as "The Children of the Veil" last night. Led by 35-year-old Everett resident Malcom Mitchell, the raid, prompted by allegations of drug use, kidnapping, and runaways, has brought to light a series of disturbing practices.

Acting on a tip from a former member, the police executed a search warrant on the secluded property on the outskirts of Everett. Law enforcement officials, accompanied by child protective services, entered the compound to investigate claims of illegal activities and ensuring the safety of the members, particularly the children.

During the raid, authorities discovered:

*- **Drugs and Paraphernalia**: Large quantities of hallucinogenic substances, including mushrooms and LSD, were found. These substances were allegedly used in the group's rituals to induce altered states of consciousness as part of their attempts to connect with a parallel dimension they referred to as the Veil.*

*- **Runaways and Addicts**: Several individuals, identified as runaways and known addicts, were living within the compound. These individuals claimed they had joined the cult seeking refuge and spiritual enlightenment, but were subjected to bizarre and potentially harmful experiments.*

*- **Experimental Practices**: Evidence of Malcom Mitchell's experimentation with body trading was uncovered. According to witnesses, Mitchell believed he could transfer souls between bodies, a practice that reportedly left participants with severe psychological repercussions.*

*- **Child Protective Services Intervention**: Among the residents was Mitchell's 10-year-old daughter. Given the concerning environment, she was immediately taken into protective custody.*

Mitchell's daughter was placed in the care of child protective services while authorities investigated the cult's activities. However, despite the alarming findings, law enforcement officials could not gather sufficient evidence to press charges against Malcom Mitchell. As a result, she was eventually returned to her father's custody.

Malcom Mitchell vehemently denied any wrongdoing, claiming that the substances found were used purely for spiritual purposes and that the individuals living on the compound were there of their own free will. He described the body trading experiments as "misunderstood spiritual practices" aimed at achieving higher states of consciousness.

The raid and its findings have sparked widespread concern among residents and advocacy groups. Critics argue that the lack of conclusive evidence and the subsequent return of the minor to her father highlight significant gaps in the system meant to protect vulnerable individuals. Mental health professionals have also expressed alarm over the potential long-term effects on those subjected to the group's experimental practices.

Despite the controversy, "The Children of the Veil" maintains a loyal following, with members continuing to support Malcom Mitchell and his teachings. The raid, while temporarily disrupting their activities, did not deter the pursuit of their spiritual goals.

As of now, the compound remains under close observation, with authorities and child protective services monitoring for any further signs of illegal activity or harm. The case remains a reminder of the challenges faced in addressing the complexities of fringe groups and protecting vulnerable individuals within such communities.

For Mitchell's daughter, her early years within the cult's confines and the subsequent raid have undoubtedly left an indelible mark. The community continues to watch with bated breath, hoping that the shadow of the Veil will eventually lift, revealing the truth behind the group and its practices.

Dom leaned back in his chair, absorbing the information. His office was sparsely decorated, with work-related files and notes scattered around. He caught fleeting glimpses of Lily in the mirrors and reflective surfaces, her image there for just a moment before vanishing. The reflections were brief but vivid, leaving him questioning his sanity.

"What are you trying to tell me, Lily?" he muttered to himself. He felt a growing connection to her, sensing desperation and fear all around him.

Dom's eyes drooped as he pushed his chair back and stood up, feeling the air pressure shift around him. He needed a moment to clear his head and made his way down the hall. As his hand trailed along the walls, he let the tactile senses ground him. The only light came from a distant, flickering bulb, casting shifting shadows on the floor. The air was cooler here, carrying a faint, musty smell mingled with the lingering aroma of cleaning chemicals.

Dom's eyes felt heavy, the strain of staring at his laptop screen for hours making them ache. He rubbed his temples and tried to shake off the weariness. Without bothering to turn on the lights, he pushed open the bathroom door and welcomed the darkness, hoping it would soothe his tired eyes.

Moonlight filtered through a small window, casting a faint, silvery glow over the tiled floor. The night was still making his skin prickle. He approached the sink and turned on the tap, the sound of running water breaking the silence. Leaning over, he splashed his face, the cold water shocking his senses awake.

As he straightened up, he glimpsed movement in the mirror. His heart skipped a beat, and he froze, staring at his reflection. For a moment, everything was silent.

Then he saw her standing behind him.

The reflection stood behind him, eyes wide with fear and desperation. Her skin was pale, almost translucent in the moonlight, and her hair hung in damp, dark strands around her face. She looked as if she had been crying, her eyes hollow and haunted.

Dom's breath caught in his throat. He spun around, but the restroom was empty, the shadows undisturbed. His pulse pounded in his ears as he turned back to the mirror. The girl was still there, her eyes locking onto his, filled with a silent plea.

He reached out to the mirror, his hand trembling. The cold glass met his fingertips, but her image remained just out of reach. Her presence was unsettling, more real than any apparition should be. She didn't speak, but her eyes conveyed a deep, unbearable sorrow.

Dom's heart raced, the air around him feeling heavier with each passing second. He tried to convince himself it was a trick of the light, a figment of his exhausted mind, but the intensity of her gaze made it impossible to dismiss.

The reflection flickered, and she vanished, leaving only his own wild-eyed face staring back at him. The room was silent once more, the shadows no longer shifting. He was alone.

Dom's breath shuddered as he backed away from the sink, his pulse still racing. The girl's desperate eyes haunted him, a message lingering in his mind. He knew this wasn't something he could ignore. She was reaching out from somewhere, and he had to find her.

CHAPTER 10

June 20, 2019

It isn't until Thursday that I look at Taylor's list. My nights are full of bad dreams (even Luke says maybe we should cool it with the lucid dreaming for a bit). So when I look at it—a perfect alternate world challenge less than 30 minutes away—I am ecstatic. So much so that I pick up the phone and call Taylor.

"Hello?" Her voice is groggy. Taylor doesn't have to work. I think her inheritance gives her the opportunity to just focus on school (she only takes one class a quarter). In a way, I am jealous, but also it just seems stagnant. Like, isn't she bored? She doesn't talk much about her hobbies in the way I share my love of the paranormal. I do at least know she is a Gemini.

"I just saw the Lake 40 Challenge!" My voice is chipper. In fact, I have been up since 5 a.m. and have already drunk three cups of coffee. I am trying to find every bit of information that I can. There isn't much to go on. Maybe it is still pretty young. Adapted by some Skykomish myth or something.

"Oh?" Taylor laughs, a sharp edge to her voice as she comes to life. "I gave you that sooo long ago."

"I know I was behind at school. I'm trying to do better in that department."

She makes some sort of dismissive noise in acknowledgment, then continues, "So, do you have class today?"

"I do, but I am free tomorrow if you want to help me figure this out."

"The instructions are right there!" she says, her tone condescending.

"I know, but..."

"But what?" she asks, a hint of impatience creeping in.

"I've never been hiking..."

Taylor bursts out laughing, a bit too loudly. "You nut. Of course, I'll help. I've done the Lake 40 trail—it's not too bad, but may be a lot for a beginner. Maybe we should hike it together first?"

"That would be great!"

"We can get you some good hiking boots—footwear is important. And a headlamp since you are going to have to do this at night. Then maybe Saturday we can do a trial hike!"

"I have to work!"

"Call in sick," she says, as if it were the most obvious solution.

I never call in sick. It's against my blood and work ethic, but I am tempted for this. "I'll think about it."

We hang up, and I look at the clock. 9:15. I should head out the door for class—it's at least a 30-minute walk, but I see my mirrors from the Fade ritual in the corner. If I don't lose time again, it should only take 15 minutes. I set them up.

As I light the candle and sit in the middle of the triangle, the air grows colder. I begin the incantation: "Into the Fade, I go. Beyond the veil, show me what I need to know." My voice is steady, but the room feels alive with an unseen presence. By the third recitation, the candle flickers, casting wild shadows on the walls.

The whispers start, faint and indistinct at first, growing louder and more insistent. Shapes move in the mirrors—flickering shadows that seem to watch me. I feel like I am being watched and close my eyes, but the whispers continue, echoing the same phrases from my dreams: "Wake up," they chant, "Wake up!"

The temperature drops further, and a shadowy figure appears in the gilded mirror. My heart races, the oppressive atmosphere pressing in on me. The shapes in the mirrors become more defined, their forms threatening. I feel a chill, like icy fingers brushing against my skin.

Everything stops. The whispers cease, and the shadows disappear, leaving the room in silence. I open my eyes, disoriented and breathless. The candle flame steadies, casting a warm glow, but the sense of being watched is stronger than ever.

Something is lingering, watching from the shadows. I didn't lose time, so I can get to school. I lock my door and head down the road. Behind me, there are footsteps, and I am afraid to look. Is the shadow following me? But it's mid-morning, and people are out and about—that would just be strange.

When turn to look, nothing is there. Yet, the unease lingers, a whisper of dread at the back of my mind. I shake it off, trying to focus on the day ahead.

The walk to school is uneventful, but my senses are heightened, every sound amplified. A bird's chirp becomes a startling cry, and the rustle of leaves sounds like hushed whispers. By the time I reach campus, I'm exhausted, my mind racing with thoughts of the Fade and what might lurk just beyond the veil.

In the middle of class, my phone buzzes with a notification from Discord. It's Luke.

ArdentElan: Hey You!

DreamSeeker: Hi! I've missed you. Tried the Fade again this morning. The whispers were louder, and I saw a shadow figure in the mirror.

ArdentElan: Sounds intense. Did you lose time again?

DreamSeeker: No, but the sense of being watched is stronger. I can't shake it.

ArdentElan: That's creepy. Maybe we should take a break from these rituals too? It's sounding dangerous.

DreamSeeker: I know, but I can't stop. I need to understand what's happening.

ArdentElan: Just be careful. Document everything. And if it gets too much, pull back.

DreamSeeker: I will. Thanks, Luke.

ArdentElan: Anytime. Stay safe.

Our leaves me feeling both reassured and anxious.

The rest of the day passes in a blur. By the time I get home, I'm exhausted, but I can't stop thinking about the Lake 40 Challenge. I'm even tempted to call in sick on Saturday to go shopping.

That evening, I find myself back in front of the mirrors again. The allure of the unknown is too strong. I light the candle and begin the ritual once more, my voice steady despite the fear gnawing at the edges of my mind.

"Into the Fade, I go. Beyond the veil, show me what I need to know."

CHAPTER 11

October 18, 2019

Dom had not slept at all the night before. Dark circles hung under his eyes, and his mind felt foggy. He sucked down his coffee as he scanned his emails, hoping the caffeine would jolt him into wakefulness. His phone buzzed, showing another message from ArdentElan on Lily's account: "Curiosity killed the cat. Be careful where you poke your nose."

These messages were getting annoying. Every note seemed designed to taunt him, to test his patience. The condescending tone gnawed at his nerves, each message a needle pricking his already frayed temper. He knew he should be the bigger person, maintain his composure, and not let the provocations get to him. Professionalism and calm would serve him better.

But exhaustion and frustration clouded his judgment. His grip tightened around the phone. He resisted the urge to throw it across the room. Instead, he typed, "Let's meet—or are you a coward?" The snarky response echoed his inner turmoil, more befitting a petulant teenager than a seasoned detective. He hit send and stared at the screen, waiting for a reply that never came.

When he arrived at the college, Dom made his way to Professor Jameson's office in Gray Wolf Hall. These institutions, often overshadowed by their larger counterparts, housed professors who were just as passionate about their subjects. In the quiet corners of these campuses, you could find scholars with profound knowledge and a genuine desire to educate. They brought a wealth of real-world experience and unique perspectives to their teaching.

The professor's office was at the end of the hall. Dom knocked on the door, which was ajar. A deep, calm voice responded, "Come in."

He pushed the door open and stepped inside. The room was a cluttered sanctuary of books, manuscripts, and curiosities from various eras. Shelves overflowed with texts on history and psychology. A large desk dominated the room, behind which sat Professor Jameson—a tall, thin man with graying hair. His eyes were sharp and inquisitive as he looked up from a stack of papers.

"Detective Dupont, I presume?" Jameson said, rising to shake Dom's hand.

"Yes, Professor. Thank you for seeing me on such short notice," Dom replied, taking a seat.

"I understand you have questions about the Children of the Veil," Jameson said, settling back into his chair. "A rather dark chapter in our local history."

"That's right. I've been investigating a case that might have ties to the group," Dom began. "I need to understand their beliefs and practices. Anything you can tell me could be helpful."

Jameson nodded, a thoughtful expression crossing his face. "The Children of the Veil were a peculiar group. Believe it or not, their origins trace back several centuries. This group evolved from various fringe religious movements that believed in accessing parallel dimensions. They believed that by crossing the 'Veil,' they could gain knowledge and power."

"How did they plan to cross this 'Veil'?" Dom asked, leaning forward.

"Their methods were... unorthodox, to say the least," Jameson said, adjusting his glasses. "They used hallucinogenic substances to induce altered states of consciousness. These rituals often involved chanting, symbolic gestures, and sometimes more disturbing practices like body trading—where they believed they could transfer souls between bodies."

Dom's mind flashed to the reports he had read. "Body trading? That sounds dangerous."

"Indeed," Jameson agreed. "Malcolm Mitchell, the leader of the Children of the Veil, was fascinated with this concept. He believed that by transferring souls, one could gain immortality or at least extend life. Unfortunately, these practices had severe psychological repercussions on those involved."

Dom's thoughts raced. "What about their structure and hierarchy? How was the group organized?"

"Mitchell was at the top, revered almost as a prophet. Below him were various levels of followers and their children, each with specific roles in their rituals and daily life. They were very secretive, bound by oaths of silence. The group disbanded after Mitchell's death, but remnants of their teachings still linger."

"And what happened to the children within the group?" Dom asked, thinking of Taylor.

"Children were often indoctrinated from a young age, taught to believe as the group did. Mitchell's own daughter, for example, was a practitioner of his teachings. After the raid on their compound, she was taken into protective custody but returned to her father's care because of insufficient evidence of abuse. The psychological impact on her must have been profound."

Dom felt a chill as he recalled the haunted look in Taylor's eyes. "Do you know if any of these children continued the work?"

Jameson sighed, a look of sadness in his eyes. "It's possible. Children raised in such environments often struggle to break free from the beliefs instilled in them. Some might even try to resurrect the group's practices, seeking to continue what they were taught was a sacred mission."

Dom hesitated for a moment, then asked, "Did you know Taylor went to school here?"

Jameson's lips thinned "Yes, I knew. Taylor was one of my students. A bright mind."

Dom's eyes narrowed. "Is she still involved in the Children of the Veil? How was she affected by all this?"

Jameson leaned back in his chair, a thoughtful expression crossing his face. "I'm happy to share what I know about the cult's doctrines and practices, but I must respect the individuals' privacy. We're not here to talk about Taylor. My knowledge is about the group."

Dom understood the delicate balance Jameson was trying to maintain. "Do you have any records or documents? Anything that might give me more insight into their rituals and beliefs?"

Jameson agreed. "I have some copies of their writings and ritual texts. They make for interesting reading, but might provide the clues you need." He stood and retrieved a three ringed binder from a shelf, handing it to Dom. "This is a transcription of one of their key texts. You can have it."

Dom took the document. "This could be very helpful," he said.

Then he thanked Jameson again and left the office, the binder clutched in his hand. As he walked back to his car, the campus now bustling with students, he couldn't help but feel a sense of urgency mixed with foreboding.

Dom glanced around, seeing the faces full of promise and potential, and wondered how many of them carried hidden scars or secret fears. The thought of Taylor among them, navigating her own internal battles while trying to appear normal. He knew the information in the binder could be a helpful tool in the investigation. It was a way to understanding the cult's lasting influence and finding those still entangled in its web.

As he reached his car, a group of students ran past him, nearly knocking the binder out of his hand. One of them shouted an apology over his shoulder. He opened the car door and slid into the driver's seat, placing the binder beside him.

"Well, at least they didn't spill my coffee," he muttered to himself, taking a sip from his thermos. The moment lifted his spirits.

Back at the station, Dom and Lauren gathered in the conference room. The binder lay open on the table between them, its pages covered in photocopied text.

"This is from Professor Jameson," Dom said, tapping the journal. "It contains detailed accounts of the Children of the Veil's rituals and beliefs."

Lauren leaned in, her eyes scanning the pages. "Nice find."

Hours passed as they pored over the journal, deciphering the references. The rituals described were more than just eccentric—they were dangerous, blurring the lines between reality and the unknown.

One passage caught Dom's attention:

"To cross the Veil, one must surrender completely, body and soul, to the unknown. The journey requires a guide, one who has walked the path before. Together, they must perform the Rite of Transference, invoking the spirits of the Veil to open the gateway. Only then can the secrets of the beyond be revealed."

He exchanged a glance with Lauren. "This one sounds ominous."

Lauren's expression was serious. "And it explains a lot about the lengths they will go. This isn't just some harmless exploration of the unknown—they believed they were unlocking powerful secrets."

Dom leaned back. "Lets keep looking."

Lauren agreed, flipping through the journal. "There's another section here on the hierarchy within the group."

Hours passed as they continued to pore over the journal, piecing together the group's history

When they had got all they could from the journal, Dom got up to refill his coffee. The break room was quiet, the hum of the fluorescent lights the only sound. He filled his mug, the bitter aroma mingling with the smell of stale donuts. His stomach growled, but he ignored it. There was no time for food.

Returning to his desk, Dom pulled up the archives database. The department was digitizing all the records, but it was a tedious task. He typed in "Malcom Mitchell 2008," and it pulled up a case number for the raid: File Number: 2008-0312-0021. A note indicated that this report had been filed and was available for review in the Records Division. This file had yet to be digitized.

With a sigh, Dom stood up and headed toward the archives. The hallway was long and lined with closed doors and the air smelled of disinfectant.

At the Records Division, he signed in at the front desk. The administrator, a middle-aged woman with reading glasses perched on her nose, glanced at him over the rim.

"Need to pull a file?" she asked.

"Yeah, case number 2008-0312-0021," Dom replied, handing over his ID.

She typed the number into her computer. "Give me a moment."

Dom waited, tapping his foot as she disappeared into the back room. Minutes later, she returned with a thick manila folder.

"Here you go. Please sign the logbook."

Dom scrawled his signature on the logbook and took the folder to a nearby table. He sat down and opened the file. Inside were detailed reports, photographs, and evidence logs.

File Number: 2008-0312-0021

Date of Report: March 13, 2008

Incident Report

Date/Time of Incident: March 12, 2008, approximately 22:30 hours

Location: Lowell Larimar Road, Everett, WA

Nature of Incident: Coordinated raid on the compound of "The Children of the Veil" based on allegations of drug use, kidnapping, and harboring runaways.

Search Warrant Issued By: Judge William Thompson, Snohomish County Superior Court

Participants:

- Everett Police Department

- Snohomish County Sheriff's Office

- Child Protective Services (CPS)

- Special Response Team (SRT)

Objective:

To investigate allegations of illegal activities, ensure the safety of individuals on the premises, and secure evidence related to the reported crimes.

Details of the Incident:

Upon entry to the compound, law enforcement officers encountered multiple individuals, including adults and minors. All individuals were detained and secured for questioning. The following items and evidence were discovered during the search:

- **Drugs and Paraphernalia:**

  - Large quantities of mushrooms, LSD, and various other hallucinogenic substances found in the primary residence and several outbuildings.

  - Drug paraphernalia was confiscated.

- **Runaways and Addicts:**

  - Six individuals identified as runaways and known addicts were residing within the compound. These individuals were taken into custody for further investigation and medical evaluation.

- **Experimental Practices:**

  - Written records and physical evidence showing experimentation with body trading were discovered. These records suggested that Malcom Mitchell, the cult leader, believed he could transfer souls between bodies, reportedly leading to severe psychological repercussions for participants.

- **Child Protective Services Intervention:**

  ○ One minor, identified as [REDACTED] (age 10), daughter of Malcom Mitchell, was found on the premises. CPS took immediate custody of the minor due to the concerning environment and potential risk to her well-being.

Statements:

Several adults residing at the compound provided statements indicating that they participated in the cult's activities willingly. They described the use of hallucinogens as part of spiritual rituals to connect with a parallel dimension known as the Veil. Witnesses confirmed experimental practices aimed at soul transfer, which resulted in mental distress for some participants.

Outcome:

Despite the discovery of drugs, paraphernalia, and evidence of experimental practices, law enforcement officials could not gather sufficient evidence to press charges against Malcom Mitchell. The minor taken into protective custody was returned to her father's care after a thorough investigation yielded inconclusive results. The cult's operations were temporarily disrupted, but no arrests were made at the time of the raid.

Follow-Up:

- The compound remains under surveillance by local authorities.

- Child Protective Services will continue to monitor the welfare of the minor.

- Further investigation into the activities of "The Children of the Veil" is ongoing.

Report Prepared By:

Officer Jeff Smith, Badge #8653

Approved By:

Sergeant Michael Johnson, Badge #2424

Confidentiality Notice:

This report contains confidential information and is intended for law enforcement use only. Unauthorized dissemination of this report is prohibited.

Dom tucked the file under his arm and headed back to his desk, bumping into Lauren on the way. She looked exhausted, her eyes ringed with dark circles similar to his own.

He held up the file. "Got the original raid reports. It's not looking good, though. Lack of conclusive evidence is a recurring theme."

Lauren grimaced. "That guy is slipperier than an eel. What are you planning next?"

"Well, not so much anymore since he is dead.." Dom smirked. "I'm going to review these and see if there's anything I missed. I might reach out to the arresting officer, in case he has insights that didn't make it into the report."

"Good idea," Lauren agreed, her voice weary.

"Let's hope so," Dom said. "You okay?"

Lauren narrowed her eyes and grumbled, "Fine."

They walked back together in silence, not speaking again until they were back at their desks.

"Can I see?" Lauren asked.

He handed her the police report. She scanned it, nodding now and then. "Kid has to be Taylor," she stated matter-of-factly.

"Yep," Dom agreed. "You gotta wonder what kind of messed-up life she had—it's no surprise she's dodgy."

Lauren sighed, her expression softening. "I messaged her again this morning, but no reply. We could just head to her house?"

Dom shook his head. "Give her another day. If she knows anything, we're more likely to get her to open up if we build that trust."

Lauren looked at him. "Agreed."

As Dom settled into his chair, Lauren's phone buzzed, and she stepped away to take the call. Dom watched her pace back and forth, her tone low and intense. He couldn't make out what she was saying, but the conversation seemed serious. When she returned, her face was a mask of frustration.

"Everything okay?" Dom asked, his concern genuine.

Lauren hesitated. "Yeah, just some personal stuff. Let's focus on the case."

Dom didn't want to push, but he also couldn't ignore the signs. "Lauren, you sure? You know you can talk to me if you need to."

She looked at him, her tough exterior cracking for a moment. "It's complicated, Dom. Let's just stick to the case."

Dom held up his hands in a placating gesture. "Alright, alright. Just checking in."

Lauren took a deep breath, her shoulders slumping. "Sorry, it's just... a lot going on."

He understood the unspoken layers in her words. "I get it."

Lauren returned to the file, her eyes scanning the pages but her mind elsewhere. Dom knew better than to push further. He glanced at her now and then and felt a pang of concern for his partner. She worked hard and kept a lot bottled inside. He resolved to tread carefully, knowing that trust, both with Taylor and his partner, was something he couldn't afford to break.

Eyes drooping, Dom pushed his chair back and stood up. The air pressure seemed to shift around him. He needed a moment to clear his head. Making his way down the hall, the shadows in the hallway stretched out like grasping fingers.

His hand trailed along walls that were lined with faded paper that had long since lost its color. The only light came from a distant, flickering bulb that cast eerie, shifting shadows on the floor. It was cooler here and the air carried a faint, musty smell that mingled with the lingering aroma of cleaning chemicals.

The strain of staring at his laptop screen for hours had been making his eyes ache. He rubbed them with the back of his hand, trying to shake off the weariness, then pushed open the restroom door. He did not bother to turn on the lights, hoping the darkness would soothe his tired eyes.

Sunlight filtered through a small, high window, casting a light over the tiled floor. The room was still, making his skin prickle. He approached the sink and turned on the tap, the sound of running water breaking the silence. Leaning over, he splashed his face, the cold water shocking his senses awake.

As he straightened up, he glimpsed movement in the mirror. His heart skipped a beat, and he froze, staring at his reflection. For a moment, everything was silent.

Then he saw her standing behind him.

The reflection of a young Asian girl stood behind him, eyes wide with fear and desperation. Her skin was pale, almost translucent in the, and her hair hung in damp, dark strands around her face. She looked as if she had been crying, her eyes hollow and haunted.

Dom's breath caught in his throat. He spun around, but the restroom was empty, the shadows undisturbed. His pulse pounded in his ears as he turned back to the mirror. The girl was still there, her eyes locking onto his, filled with a silent plea.

He reached out to the mirror, his hand trembling. The cold glass met his fingertips, but her image remained just out of reach. Her presence was unsettling, more real than any apparition should be. She didn't speak, but her eyes conveyed a deep, unbearable sorrow.

Dom's heart raced, the air around him feeling heavier with each passing second. He tried to convince himself it was a trick of the light, a figment of his exhausted mind, but the intensity of her gaze made it impossible to dismiss.

The reflection flickered, and she vanished, leaving only his own wide-eyed face staring back at him. The restroom was empty once more, the shadows no longer shifting. He was alone.

Dom's breath shuddered as he backed away from the sink, his pulse still racing. He looked up, catching his reflection in the mirror. The circles under his eyes stood out, telling the story of too many sleepless nights spent chasing shadows.

He took a moment to steady himself, running a hand over his short-cropped hair and straightening his shirt. With a deep breath, he turned away from the mirror and walked back to his desk.

As he sat down, he forced himself to appear calm, pretending nothing had just happened. He organized the notes and files spread out before him. This investigation was getting to him, but he would not let it show. Not now. Not when he was so close to the answers he needed.

Chapter 12

June 23, 2019

I resisted calling in because I still need to pay rent. This week, I've been good at showing up for work. Go me! Yesterday was slow for a Saturday. I've taken to avoiding mirrors. I do the ritual daily now, and I've found that whenever I look into any mirror, something is off. It's like there's something behind me, just out of sight. I see a shadow or the whisper of a hand, but when I turn around, nothing is there.

I was distracted by the store's fluorescent lights buzzing overhead. They cast long, unnatural shadows that seem to move on their own. The air feels thicker there, more oppressive. It's as if the atmosphere is charged with something unseen, something evil. At one point, I was stocking shelves and heard my name whispered from the next aisle. I rushed over, heart pounding, but no one was there. It's not the first time that happened, and I know it won't be the last. These incidents only fuel my obsession, reinforcing the feeling that I'm on the brink of discovering something monumental. My coworkers think I am an oddball, and I can't blame them. I'm jumpy, distracted, always looking over my shoulder.

Each day, the line between the real and the unreal blurs more. It consumes my thoughts. The rituals and whispers in the dark are relentless. All I can think about is the Lake 40 Challenge. Work feels like another world, distant and unimportant, something I should care about but can't bring myself to.

I'm off today. It's a good day to catch up on errands, but I let Taylor take me to REI. She is enthusiastic, almost more than I am. We hit the outdoor store, and she takes charge, picking out the best headlamp, hiking poles, and various safety gear. At one point, I catch that odd glint in her eye again. It's unsettling, but I'm grateful for her help. She even offers to drive us to the trailhead the day I do the ritual—a gesture that feels both kind and possessive.

"You know it has to be done solo, right?" I remind her, trying to gauge her reaction.

"Yes... I'm aware of that," she rolls her eyes. "You also don't have a car, and this place is out in the middle of bumfuck nowhere..."

I laugh. She's not wrong, and if she's offering, I'll save money on the Uber I was going to order.

"Plus," she continues. "It says nothing about going solo on a practice hike, does it? As the more experienced hiker of the two of us, I elect myself to train you."

"Okay, okay!" I laugh again, but there's a slight edge to it. "You win!"

Later, when I'm alone at home, I think of Luke. Even though he suggested chilling on the Fade ritual, he's supportive of this. That being said, he seems to change the subject every time I mention Lake 40. It's as if he's scared and won't admit it. He's probably right to worry. I have done no actual work in days, and the guilt gnaws at me. But the pull of the paranormal is too strong to ignore. My tasks lie abandoned, gathering dust. Every time I try to focus, my mind drifts back to the rituals, the whispers, the shadows.

Night falls, and I lie in bed, staring at the ceiling. Shadows dance in the corners of my room, and I wonder if they're real or just figments of my exhausted mind. I turn over, trying to shake the unease. Tomorrow is another day. The Lake 40 Challenge is looming, and with it, the promise of answers—or more questions. I'm ready for whatever comes, or at least that's what I tell myself as I drift into a restless sleep, the line between my dreams and reality becoming ever more tenuous.

I hear a tapping at the window. When I turn to look, nothing is there. Yet, the unease lingers, a whisper of dread at the back of my mind. I shake it off, trying to focus on sleep. Just as I am about to drift into oblivion, my phone buzzes.

Taylor texts me a brief message that pulls me back to reality: "Ready for the practice hike Saturday? I can't wait."

It's after midnight, but she has no classes or nowhere to be. I could always ignore it; she would understand, but I reply: "Yes. I'm excited. I have the next two Saturdays off."

Her response is almost immediate: "Good. See you then."

I put my phone upside down and attempt to go to sleep again, but it's no use. My mind is spinning.

As I lie there, I think about the ritual steps, imagining myself walking the trail, feeling the cool night air on my skin, hearing the distant cry of a baby by the lake. What will I see in the water? What will I hear? The anticipation is almost unbearable. My thoughts drift back to the moments in the store, the whispered voice, the shadows. Are they connected to the same place? Is this just my mind playing tricks on me, or is there something more sinister at work?

I glance at the mirror across the room, the reflection barely visible in the dim light. For a moment, I think I see a movement behind me, a flicker of a shadow. I turn my head, but there's nothing there. Just the silent, empty room. I need to stop this. I need to focus on what's real.

But as I close my eyes, the feeling of being watched, of something lurking just out of sight, remains. And with that, I drift into an uneasy sleep.

CHAPTER 13

October 21, 2019

Dom Dupont walked into the briefing room, the aroma of his coffee mingling with the faint scent of dry-erase markers. The no-frills space seemed to hum with an undercurrent of urgency. Plain white walls, punctuated by a few commendation plaques, reflected the stark overhead lighting. His gaze drifted to the large corkboard crammed with case notes and photos, each piece a fragment of the puzzles he lived to solve. The rectangular table in the center, ringed by worn chairs, was already strewn with files. At one end of the room, the whiteboard displayed the day's agenda in scrawled handwriting, while the clock above the doorway ticked away, a relentless reminder that every second counted.

He took a seat beside Lauren, who was already flipping through a stack of case files. The other detectives and officers filled in around them, murmuring among themselves.

As Dom turned to speak to Lauren, his eyes caught a dark bruise on her forearm, hidden by the sleeve of her shirt. It was a deep, angry mark, the result of a forceful grip. His heart sank, and a familiar anger flared within him. He had seen similar bruises countless times in his career—evidence of abuse, of someone being hurt by those who were supposed to care for them.

When he tried to meet Lauren's eyes, she looked away. Dom's jaw clenched.

"You, me, conversation after this," he stated, his voice low and firm.

She just sighed, her shoulders slumping. Dom recognized the signs all too well—the subtle avoidance, the quiet endurance of pain. He'd seen it in victims of domestic violence, people who were too proud or too scared to ask for help. The shame of a cop being in such a situation was written all over her downcast eyes and tight-lipped silence.

Sergeant Robert Anders was a no-nonsense leader with years of experience. Dom didn't know him well, but had heard enough to respect him. Anders commanded the room, his presence alone enough to silence the murmurs of conversation.

The sergeant drew everyone's attention with a sharp, practiced ease. "Alright, let's get started," he began.

Dom settled in, keen to keep his head down and observe. As the newest member of the force, he was still finding his footing, and meetings like this were as much about learning the ropes as they were about contributing.

Ander's gaze swept across the room. "We've got a busy day ahead," he continued, "and we need all hands on deck."

Ray Collins stepped forward, holding a tablet. "We received detailed results from the lab on the evidence collected from the Lake 40 site. All the blood found at the scene was animal blood. No human DNA was detected. Normally, this would close the case, but given the ties to the Lily Chen, we're keeping it open."

Sergeant Anders nodded. "Good work, Collins. Now, what about the latest from Lily Chen's laptop?"

Collins tapped his tablet, bringing up the relevant files. "We found several chat logs about the Lake 40 Challenge. Lily was involved in researching and discussing this challenge with various online communities. It seems she was planning to perform the ritual herself." This is corroborated by the journal. Johnson turned his attention to Dom and Lauren. "Dupont, Kim, what's your take on this?"

Dom straightened in his chair. "Agreed, and witness statements place her last known location at the Lake 40 Trailhead. While doing a background history on Taylor, we connected her to Malcolm Mitchell, the leader of the

Children of the Veil, who is now deceased. Further research revealed ties between the group and this location."

"Evidence suggests the cult believed the Lake 40 area was a gateway to a parallel dimension they called the Veil. We're following up on leads that connect the cult to the Lake 40 Challenge. We are still attempting to arrange a meeting with Taylor Mitchell without having to resort to a subpoena."

Anders raised an eyebrow. "Interesting. Make sure you handle that meeting carefully. Her insights could be crucial. Anything else?"

Lauren chimed in, "We're also planning to visit the Lake 40 Trailhead during the day to gather more evidence firsthand. We believe there might be something we missed during the initial sweep."

"Understood. Stay safe out there. Now, for new assignments. Collins, you're on the follow-up for the robbery case from yesterday. The rest of you, check your emails for detailed instructions on your tasks for today."

After writing a few notes on the whiteboard, the sergeant turned back to the group. "Remember, we've got a lot of eyes on us with these high-profile cases. Keep your reports thorough and timely. And if anyone has any issues or needs help, ask. That's it for now. Let's get to work."

The detectives and officers dispersed, gathering their things and heading out to their assignments. Lauren made a beeline for the ladies' room.

"Don't think I've forgotten," Dom called after her.

"I just have to pee, geez!" Lauren shot back, rolling her eyes.

Dom waited outside the bathroom door. A couple of officers passing by gave him quizzical looks, to which he responded with a shrug and a grin.

"Guard duty," he joked.

Lauren emerged a moment later, looking more composed. Dom gestured toward the parking lot. "We're heading to the medical examiner's office. We can talk on the way."

Lauren fell into step beside him as they walked toward the parking lot.

"Don't you think you're overreacting?" she asked, trying to keep her tone light.

"Not when it comes to my partner's well-being," Dom replied, giving her a sidelong glance. He could see the tension in her shoulders, the weariness in her eyes. "Now, about that bruise..."

Lauren sighed again, this time more heavily. "Alright, alright. We'll talk. Just don't go all 'detective mode' on me, okay?"

Dom slid into the driver's seat, glancing at Lauren as she settled in next to him. The car hummed to life, and he pulled out of the parking lot, heading toward the medical examiner's office.

"It was an accident—" Lauren started, but Dom cut her off.

"Don't give me that bullshit. Even if it was, it wasn't," Dom said.

Lauren rubbed her forehead, staring out the window. "She was drunk. We were fighting about my work schedule. Then it digressed into accusing me of cheating on her."

Dom shook his head, his grip tightening on the steering wheel. "When would you have time for that? You work nonstop and take care of her."

Lauren let out a bitter laugh. "She thinks it's with you."

Dom chuckled. "Is there something I don't know about you? Have you decided to try men for a while?"

Lauren smacked his arm. "No, she's just scared I'm going to leave her. This lets her play the victim. But I won't leave her."

"Maybe you should," Dom suggested, glancing at her before returning his focus to the road.

"She needs me," Lauren replied.

Dom raised an eyebrow. "You know, Lauren, you're hurting her more than helping her. She's never going to get better if you keep propping her up."

Lauren shrugged. "I can't just abandon her."

"It's not abandoning," Dom said. "Sometimes the best way to help someone is to let them stand on their own. She needs to face her issues, not hide behind you."

Lauren was silent for a moment, processing his words. She looked at Dom. "I know you're right," she admitted. "But it's just so hard."

Dom reached over, giving her hand a squeeze. "I'm here for you, Lauren. Whatever you decide, I've got your back. But think about what's best for both of you."

"Thanks."

Dom parked outside the Snohomish County Superior Court, his thoughts drifting back to New Orleans. The sleek, modern design of the Everett courthouse, with its clean lines and glass facade, contrasted with the historical grandeur of New Orleans' judicial buildings.

As they stepped out of the car, Dom couldn't help but compare the two. The Lousianna Supreme Court, where he'd spent many days early in his career, was a masterpiece. Its architecture gave it an air of timelessness that the contemporary design of this building lacked. Yet, there was a certain efficiency to the modern courthouse that Dom appreciated, a no-nonsense practicality.

Inside was a hive of activity. The constant hum of conversations set a tone of urgency and importance. As they headed towards the courtroom, Dom turned to Lauren. "Ever been to New Orleans?" he asked, trying to lighten the mood.

She shook her head. "No, but I've always wanted to visit. I've heard it's amazing."

"It is," Dom replied. "The Cabildo, where the Louisiana Supreme Court used to be, is a piece of history. It's all grand hallways and intricate details, like stepping back in time. This place," he gestured around, "is all about modern efficiency. No frills, just function."

Lauren smiled. "I guess both have their merits. But I wouldn't mind a bit of old-world charm."

Dom chuckled. "Maybe one day this will be considered old-world charm."

"Strange thought," Lauren smiled, more relaxed than she had been all day.

When they reached the administrative wing, Dom's demeanor shifted back to professional focus. As they stepped inside, he couldn't shake the feeling of being in two worlds—one foot in his younger days as a cop in New Orleans, the other in the modern, streamlined present of Everett. It was as if his old life did not want to let him go.

Dom and Lauren stood at the counter in the records office of the Snohomish County Superior Court. The clerk handed them a manila folder containing the death certificate for Malcolm Mitchell, and a few transcripts from court cases involving the Children of the Veil.

"We have a reading room available if you need to review these documents," she offered.

"That would be helpful. We may also need to access additional court records related to the Children of the Veil. Can we request those here as well?"

"Absolutely," the clerk replied. "Follow me."

She led them to a small, quiet room equipped with a large table, chairs, and a computer terminal. The room was designed with plenty of space to spread out papers and make notes. Dom and Lauren settled in, and the clerk returned to her station. Dom scanned the death certificate.

"Date of death: July 16, 2015. Cause of death: drowning. Manner of death: suicide, with suspicions of accidental drowning noted," he read aloud.

Lauren leaned in closer, her eyes widening as she read the next line. "Place of death: Lake 40, Granite Falls, WA. That's the same place where Lily disappeared from."

Dom's mind raced, the pieces of the puzzle aligning. "According to the journal, it was Taylor that suggested this hike to Lily. I find it odd she would send her friend to the same place her father died."

"Things don't add up," Lauren said. "I think we need to stop being patient and confront Taylor Mitchell."

Just then, Lauren's phone buzzed. She glanced at the screen, her eyebrows shooting up. "Speak of the devil... It's a text from Taylor. She says she's willing to meet but only on her terms. She gives a time and an address at a local park."

Dom's jaw tightened. "What time?"

"Tomorrow, 11 AM at Tambark Creek Park in Bothell."

"Good," Dom replied. "We have time to get through these court records first. There might be something that ties all of this together."

They began working through the files. The records detailed many incidents involving the cult, including a notable case where Malcolm Mitchell was charged with unlawful assembly, disturbing the peace, and endangering the welfare of a minor during a ritual in a secluded forest area. The file included a police report describing how officers had found the group during a midnight ritual, chanting and performing rites that Mitchell claimed were necessary to connect with a parallel dimension they called "the Veil."

"This guy was out there," Dom muttered, passing the file to Lauren. "Look at this. They had altars, symbols, the whole shebang."

Lauren's eyes were fixed on a page detailing the evidence collected from the scene: ritual paraphernalia, written texts on cult doctrine, and photographs of the group mid-ceremony that looked familiar to the scene last week at the Lake 40 trailhead. "It's like something out of a horror movie," she said, shaking her head.

Dom flipped to another page, his expression darkening. "They were also arrested for animal cruelty."

Lauren just shook her head.

The next file was a court transcript from a 2014 trial. Mitchell had been charged with disturbing the peace and unlawful assembly after another incident in a rural area. The transcript detailed testimonies from residents who had heard eerie chanting and seen strange lights in the woods at night. One witness described seeing figures in hooded robes carrying lanterns along a hidden path.

"This isn't just casual interest," Dom said, frowning. "Mitchell was committed. And look at this—he defended himself in court, claiming that their rituals were peaceful and meant to bring enlightenment."

Lauren glanced at the judge's ruling, which had fined Mitchell and issued a restraining order barring him from practicing religious ceremonies in certain public lands. "He didn't stop, though," she said. "He just found new ways to circumvent the law."

Another document was a detailed investigation report from 2015, just weeks before Mitchell's death. It included interviews with former cult members who had left the group, citing fear and disillusionment. One ex-member recounted a chilling experience where Mitchell had talked about needing a "sacrifice" to open the Veil.

Dom's stomach turned. "This guy was on a dark path. No wonder his death is so suspicious."

Lauren's eyes darkened with realization. "I wonder how much Taylor was involved."

As they gathered the documents and headed out of the reading room, Dom's phone buzzed.

ArdentElan: I see you. Look up.

Dom looked up and saw the red light of a security camera. Who was this guy, and how did he fit into the puzzle? A chill ran down his spine.

"You look like you saw a ghost," Lauren said, her voice tinged with concern.

Dom wanted to tell her. Her insight would be invaluable, but he couldn't drag her into this unknown danger. "Just my lunch not sitting well," he lied, tossing her the keys. "Meet you at the car."

He made a beeline to the restroom, his heart pounding. Inside, he splashed cold water on his face, trying to steady his nerves. When he looked up into the mirror, his breath caught in his throat. Reflected behind him was the same face of the woman in his mirror, Lily.

Dom spun around, but the restroom was empty. His pulse raced as he turned back to the mirror, half expecting her to be gone. She was still there, her expression desperate and sorrowful.

Dom took a deep breath, his mind racing. Was this some kind of hallucination? Or was it a message from the beyond? He shook his head, trying to clear his thoughts. This day had taken a turn for the bizarre, and he needed to stay focused.

He exited the restroom, glancing around to make sure he wasn't being watched. Lauren was waiting by the car.

"Everything okay?" she asked.

"Yeah," Dom replied, forcing a smile. "Just needed a moment. Let's go."

As they drove to their next destination, Dom couldn't shake the image. He didn't know who ArdentElan was or how he fit into their investigation, but one thing was clear—things were getting more complicated by the minute.

CHAPTER 14

June 27, 2019

Five days until the Lake 40 Challenge and just two before the trial hike. Taylor will be there for both, her presence a steady comfort. As I skim through the steps once more, I try to tell myself I'm not superstitious, but there's a persistent unease I can't shake. The new moon rises on Tuesday, casting its shadow over my thoughts. This weekend, Taylor and I will tackle the practice hike, and she'll drive me on the 2nd. She's more than a good friend. She's my anchor in this swirling uncertainty.

1.) Start your hike at the Lake 40 Trailhead at midnight on a moonless night.

Midnight on a moonless night—it sounds like the start of every horror movie ever.

2.) Be alone. If there's a car in the lot or people around, do not proceed.

Great, so if I see anyone, I have to chicken out.

3.) Walk steadily and don't look back.

There's something about the idea of not looking back that feels wrong. It goes against every instinct to check for danger. What if there's something behind me, just out of sight, waiting to pounce?

4.) If you hear noises or voices behind you, ignore them. Ignore them.

Sure, no problem. Just pretend I don't hear whispers in the dark.

5.) Past the 1.3-mile marker, find a moss-covered rock with a crack. Put a personal item inside.

Okay, that's specific. A moss-covered rock with a crack. Stay focused on the rock and trail. I suppose if I am terrified; it provides a focal point.

6.) At the lake, sit facing the water. Close your eyes and listen. If you don't hear a baby's cry, the ritual failed.

Do I want to hear a baby cry? I mean, I want the ritual to work. But a baby crying in the dark, alone?

7.) If you hear the cry, look into the water. Keep your gaze steady even if you see shapes or hear whispers. If a dark figure appears, you've succeeded. Avoid its eyes and don't answer its questions.

A dark figure appearing. Wonderful.

8.) Regardless of the result, leave without looking back or taking your item. Following these steps will grant you special sight, revealing hidden paths.

Okay...Then what? I guess that's what we will find out.

9.) Never share your experience. Speaking of it attracts unwelcome attention from the fade.

Right, because the fade wasn't creepy enough already. This is what I want, though. To touch the other side.

I set up my daily Fade ritual. It's like a drug to me. Now if I skip it, I feel empty and alone.

Afterward, I head to the bathroom to get ready for work. My face looks gaunt and pale in the mirror. I stare at it, wondering if I should throw on some makeup. I'm not usually a makeup person, but this is pretty bad. Then something happens. My image tilts its head ever so slightly. Did I do that? There's this gnawing feeling in the pit of my stomach. I lean in and fake a smile, showing my teeth. The image copies me.

I exhale. I'm just going a little crazy. Probably nervous about the hike alone. I question why I'm even doing this. The logical side of my brain tells me I'm going overboard with just fancying the supernatural. But it's like a drug, and I can't stop. I check my face one more time. This time, the image in the mirror brings its finger to its lips as though telling me to be quiet.

I KNOW I'm not doing that. Oh shit, oh shit. My legs feel weak. Maybe I should call in sick. But I'm already taking Saturday and Tuesday off. Tuesday was harder to get off—everyone wanted time off for the 4th of July. I promised I'd be back.

I remember my image in the mirror and my head snaps back. It's all normal again. I have the urge to smash the glass in front of me, but what good would that do? Instead, I pick up the phone to call Taylor. I thought about messaging Luke, but Taylor has always been the skeptic and voice of reason.

The phone rings twice before she answers. "Hey, what's up?"

"I think I need to bail on this Lake 40 thing. I am going crazy!"

The line is silent for a moment before Taylor replies. "Don't do that. You've been working so hard to prepare!"

I'm flabbergasted. She's the one who always thinks my ideas are wild. "Really?"

"Yeah. Let's do the hike Saturday, and if you're still feeling this way, you can reassess."

I wonder if she just wants to get me to go hiking with her. Sometimes, I think Taylor is lonelier than me. "Okay..." I whisper and look toward the bathroom. "Taylor?"

"Yes?" she answers.

"Have you ever heard of a fetch?" The line goes silent again.

"Uh... no."

A fetch is an eerie concept from Irish folklore. It's a spectral double of a living person, believed to be an omen of impending death. Seeing your own fetch means you're going to die soon. The thought sends chills down my spine, but I can't bring myself to tell Taylor that. She'd think I'm crazy, or worse, she'd worry too much.

"I think you're just letting your imagination get the best of you," Taylor says, breaking the silence.

"You're right," I reply, but the doubt lingers, gnawing at me like a shadow that won't leave. I hang up, trying to shake off the unease, but the idea of the fetch and what I saw in the mirror keeps haunting me. Maybe I am just imagining things, but what if I'm not?

Chapter 15

October 21, 2019

Dom Dupont sat at his desk, the surrounding air filled with the aroma of his Indian takeout. He took a bite of curry, savoring it as he looked around his apartment. The space was quiet, lit only by a dim desk lamp casting long shadows on the walls. Outside, the city was dark and silent, with the occasional sound of a car passing by or a distant siren breaking the stillness.

Dom's laptop hummed as he logged into Discord using Lily's credentials. His fingers moved over the keyboard, downloading the transcript of ArdentElan's server and all the private chats between Lily and ArdentElan. He leaned back in his chair, wiping his hands on a napkin before he started scrolling through the messages.

As he sifted through the chat logs, Dom noted the extensive amount of direct messages between Lily and ArdentElan, far more than her contributions to the public chat room. He frowned, seeing patterns that disturbed him—behaviors not just directed at Lily, but at other users in the server as well. His jaw tightened as he read the insidious encouragements, the subtle manipulations.

He went back to the beginning, to when Lily first joined the server. The early messages were casual, with Lily introducing herself and taking part in discussions. It was a while before ArdentElan mentioned a group called the Children of the Veil. He described it as an incredible source of knowledge and community, a group that had deep insights into the mysteries of the supernatural.

"This group is the real deal," ArdentElan had written. "They're based in Washington and have a lot of resources. You should definitely check them out if you're serious about uncovering the truth."

Dom's eyes narrowed. He knew this group—Malcolm Mitchell had led the Children of the Veil.

Scrolling further, he saw Lily's reply. Her screen name, **DreamSeeker**, stood out among the other users.

"That's near me!" she had responded. "I've heard about them. Maybe I should visit?"

It was after this comment that ArdentElan first messaged her. The conversation started innocuously enough, with Lily mentioning her excitement about going to

Everett Community College. ArdentElan responded, saying he was in community college too, creating a false sense of camaraderie and trust.

Dom's eyes narrowed as he read on, his curry growing cold beside him. The initial friendly messages shifted into more personal and probing questions. He felt a knot tightening in his stomach as he realized the extent of ArdentElan's influence over Lily and others.

About a month later, their messages showed them sharing their real names. ArdentElan introduced himself as Luke. Dom felt a chill run down his spine. This wasn't just an online predator; Luke had cultivated a relationship with Lily, guiding her toward the dangerous cult.

Dom scrolled further, hoping for a connection that tied Luke to The Children of the Veil, but found nothing.

As he continued to scroll through the messages, the room felt colder, the quiet pressing in around him. What he was uncovering settled on his shoulders. He took a deep breath, steeling himself for what he knew would be a long night of digging through the darkness to find the truth. He had a lot to understand before meeting with Taylor tomorrow.

****

Dom and Lauren pulled into the parking lot of Tambark Creek Park and exited the car. The morning sun cast a warm glow over the sprawling fields and dense woodlands. A slight breeze rustled the leaves, carrying the faint scent of pine and earth.

As they walked past the playground, the distant sounds of children laughing seemed almost alien compared to their thoughts. They followed a paved trail that wound through the trees until they found the bench they were supposed to meet at. It was empty. Dom gestured for Lauren to sit, and they both settled in.

Dom broke the silence first. "You doing okay?" he asked.

Lauren stared at the ground for a moment before speaking. "I've been thinking about what you said. About Natalie and everything."

Dom waited, sensing she needed to get this off her chest.

"You were right," Lauren continued. "I can't keep living like this. I'm thinking about giving her an ultimatum—get sober and go to therapy, or I'm out."

Dom leaned back, considering her words. "Ultimatums can backfire. They make people feel cornered."

Lauren looked up, frustration in her eyes. "What should I do then?"

Dom sighed. "Sometimes, the best thing you can do is leave. It forces her to make a choice. If she cares about you, she'll realize she needs to change. But staying and enabling her won't help either of you."

Lauren's shoulders slumped. "But we have a lease together. It's not that easy."

"I get that," Dom said. "But you gotta think of you."

Before Lauren could respond, a young woman approached them. Dom recognized her as the same woman he had seen at the college. She looked to be in her early twenties, with dark hair pulled back into a messy bun and circles under her eyes that hinted at many sleepless nights. Dressed in jeans and a hoodie, her wary expression and the way she scanned the park betrayed her nerves.

Dom stood up, looking toward the woman. "That's gotta be her," he muttered.

Lauren composed herself and rose to greet the woman. "You must be Taylor."

Taylor glanced around as if someone followed her before nodding and sitting next to them. Dom sensed a tension in the air, a sort of static charge that prickled at his instincts. There was more to this girl than met the eye, and the way she seemed to look over her shoulder gave him pause.

"It's okay," Dom assured her, trying to ease her fear. "You are not in trouble. We just want to find Lily."

Taylor's eyes were red-rimmed, as though she had been crying before she arrived. She looked like she was about to say something, but then just nodded. This girl was shaken, and Dom wasn't sure how to process it. The raw emotion in her eyes tugged at his own, making him want to protect her, to ease her fear, but he knew they needed facts.

Lauren broke the awkward silence. "Taylor, thank you for coming in. We know this is difficult, but we need your help to understand what happened to Lily. Can you tell us the last time you saw her?"

Taylor took a deep breath, her fingers twisting in her lap. "It was the night I dropped her off at the Lake 40 trailhead. She was... excited but also kind of nervous. She kept talking about this 'Lake 40 Challenge,' like it was some kind of adventure."

Dom leaned forward, his eyes narrowing as he observed Taylor's body language. She seemed genuine, but there was something more, a hesitation that hinted at deeper fears. If Lily's journal was accurate, it was Taylor who had suggested this challenge. "Did Lily say why she wanted to do this challenge?" he asked, his voice gentle but probing.

Taylor swallowed hard and glanced down at her hands. "She said it was for fun, to test herself, but I think she was looking for something. Lately, she'd been really into these weird rituals and urban legends. 'The Fade,' she called it, and she believed there might be something to it."

Why did she hide the fact she suggested it to Lily? Dom observed her for a moment before continuing.

"The Fade?" Dom echoed, exchanging a brief, signifi-cant glance with Lauren. His thoughts raced back to the journal entries, the eerie rituals, and his own unsettling experiences. "Can you tell us more about that?"

Taylor's voice trembled. "It's some kind of ritual she found on Reddit. She tried it a few times and... said she lost time. She seemed obsessed with it, like she was trying to find something beyond our world."

Dom's mind flashed to his own encounter, the cold, oppressive air in his bathroom, the vision of the woman in the mirror. He suppressed a shiver, focusing on Taylor. "Did she ever mention seeing or hearing anything unusual?"

Taylor hesitated, biting her lip. "She said she felt like she was being watched, that sometimes she heard whispers. I thought it was just her imagination, but now... I'm not so sure."

"Did you ever try any of these challenges or rituals with her?" Dom asked.

Taylor shook her head. "No, it wasn't my thing."

Dom sensed a shift in her demeanor, a subtle tightening of her posture, as if she were bracing herself. "Tell us about your father."

She went white as a ghost, stumbling over her words. "W... What does he have to do with this? He is d... dead."

"I am so sorry for your loss, but it is important. Didn't he die at Lake 40?" Dom asked, his tone gentle but insistent.

Taylor's reaction was immediate, her face contorting with anger. "What are you saying? Are you accusing—"

Lauren took over, her voice soothing. "Taylor, we are not accusing you of anything." She shot Dom a look, a silent plea for patience. "Anything you can tell us, no matter how small, could be crucial. Did Lily have any other friends she confided in? Anyone who might know more about these rituals?"

Taylor shook her head, her anger giving way to defeat. "Not really. She kept to herself mostly. I was probably the closest person she had, and even I didn't understand half of what she was into."

Dom leaned back, his mind working through the new information. The connection to Taylor's father added a layer of complexity to the case. He felt the unspoken secrets pressing down. There was something in Taylor's eyes, a flicker of fear and guilt that hinted at more than she was saying.

"Taylor," Dom began, choosing his words, "we know this is hard for you. Your father's history with Lake 40 and his organization... it's all relevant to understanding what Lily might have been involved in. We just need to know what you know."

Taylor's eyes filled with tears, and she wiped them away. "My dad... he believed in all that stuff. He dragged me into it, made me part of his rituals. I hated it. When he died, I thought I could escape it, but... it's like it never left me."

Dom felt a pang of empathy. "Did Lily know about your father? About the cult?"

Taylor shook her head, her voice barely above a whisper. "No. I didn't want her to know that part of my life. It would have been all she saw. I just wanted a friend, and I never really had any. But she was curious, thought all that stuff was fascinating…"

"We're going to find Lily," Dom said, his tone firm yet gentle. "But we need you to be completely honest with us. If there's anything else, anything at all, you need to tell us now."

Taylor took a shaky breath, her eyes darting from Lauren to Dom, her lip quivering as she bit down on it. She seemed to weigh something heavy in her mind, her fingers twitching in her lap. "My…" She hesitated, the words stuck in her throat. "My class starts soon. I need to go."

She rose abruptly; the bench creaking under the sudden shift. Dom watched her, sensing the turmoil in her movements, the way her shoulders hunched as if burdened by an invisible weight. He exchanged a quick, concerned glance with Lauren.

Taylor's footsteps were quick and uneven as she walked away, almost stumbling over the uneven path. Her fingers fumbled with the strap of her bag, clutching it to her chest. She paused, looking back at them with a mixture of fear and regret, her eyes glistening with unshed tears. Then, without another word, she turned and continued down the path; her figure soon blending into the park's greenery.

Dom let out a slow breath, running a hand through his hair. The park felt quieter without her and the tension lingered in the air. "She's holding back," he mumbled, more to himself than to Lauren.

Lauren's brow furrowed. "Definitely. There's more she's not telling us. Her connection to the cult, her father... it's all tied to Lily's disappearance. We need to get her to open up."

Dom stood up, pacing a few steps along the path. "We can't push too hard, or she'll shut down completely. But we need her to trust us, to see that we're here to help."

Lauren watched him, her expression thoughtful. "Maybe we should try a different approach. Show her we understand, that we're not just here to interrogate her."

Dom stopped pacing, meeting Lauren's eyes. "You're right. We need to build a rapport, make her feel safe. It's the only way we'll sort this out."

"Let's regroup and figure out our next move. We've got a lot of work ahead of us."

As they gathered their things, Dom couldn't shake the image of Taylor's haunted expression. The secrets she carried were a lot, and he knew they were key to unraveling Lily's disappearance. He resolved to get to the truth, no matter how deep he had to dig.

They started walking back to the car, autumn leaves crunching under their feet. Dom glanced around the park, noting how the bright colors seemed at odds with the darkness of their investigation. There were always things hidden under the surface, if you knew how to find them.

Lauren broke the silence. "Dom, do you think she's scared of something? Or someone?"

Dom considered this, his mind racing through the possibilities. "Could be. The way she reacted when we mentioned her father... there's definitely something there. We need to find out what she's so afraid of."

"Agreed. We should also look into her father's death more closely, and see if there are any active members of the cult. There might be connections we haven't seen yet."

Back at the station, they settled into their desks. Dom began digging into Taylor's background, searching for any additional details about her family and their ties to the cult.

"Lauren, can you check if there are any recent activities or members linked to the Children of the Veil?" Dom asked, his fingers flying over the keyboard.

"On it," Lauren replied, pulling up the database of known associates and recent police reports involving the cult.

Dom's search turned up an old article about Malcolm Mitchell, Taylor's father. He had been the leader of the Children of the Veil until his untimely death at Lake 40 under mysterious circumstances. The article mentioned that Taylor's mother, Evelyn Mitchell, had died shortly after Taylor was born. Dom's eyes narrowed as he read on. Raised by her father, Taylor had been immersed from a young age.

"Lauren, look at this," Dom said, turning his monitor toward her. "Taylor's mother died when she was just a baby. Her father raised her alone."

Lauren frowned, scanning the article. "So, we have a deceased mother, a father who led a cult and died mysteriously, and a daughter living alone in a house with cult ties."

"Any known members around?"

Lauren agreed. "I'll see what I can find, and cross-reference the names with any known addresses or meeting places in the area."

Dom leaned back in his chair, rubbing his temples. "Then we need to talk to Taylor again."

"Hey," Lauren said, gesturing to the computer screen. "I found some info about known cult members. Two names came up frequently: Amanda Weiss and Richard Hale. They've both been arrested recently."

Dom leaned in, his eyes scanning the data displayed on the monitor. "Do we have addresses for them?"

"Yes, Amanda Weiss lives in a house on Maple Street, and Richard Hale has been staying at a motel downtown, but he was arrested last night for public intoxication and may still be at the Snohomish County Jail."

Lauren turned to Dom. "We should split up. You take Amanda Weiss, and I'll talk to Richard Hale."

Dom agreed. "Good idea. Let's move."

As Dom drove to Maple Street, he tried to fit together all the pieces of the puzzle in his mind. Taylor's unease, the cult's shadowy presence, and the string of mysterious deaths. The afternoon light cast long, creeping shadows that seemed to writhe with a life of their own, creating an eerie atmosphere despite the early hour.

His thoughts drifted to a case in New Orleans that had given him the same unsettling feeling. He remembered a series of ritualistic murders in the French Quarter; the victims were found with strange symbols carved into their skin. The case had led him deep into the city's underbelly, uncovering an evil that thrived on fear and blood. He recalled the oppressive heat, the heavy scent of decay in the air, and the feeling of eyes watching him from the shadows. That same sense of dread now pressed down on him as he neared Amanda Weiss's townhouse.

CHAPTER 16

June 30, 2019

The hike on Saturday was incredible! If this paranormal thing doesn't work out, I think I've found my new obsession. The air was clean, and my body hadn't worked that hard in ages. Taylor was quiet; I don't recall ever seeing her like that. She seemed to be deep in thought.

Still, I am a little nervous about doing this at night (and in the dark). There were a few parts where I felt like I was rock climbing or something—but it will be okay.

My phone buzzes on the table, jolting me from my thoughts. I see Taylor's name flash on the screen. Odd, she rarely calls this early, especially on a Sunday.

"Hey, Taylor!" I answer. "What's up?"

There's a pause, and then she sighs. "Hey, Lily. I hate to do this, but I can't take you to the trailhead Tuesday. Something came up."

My heart sinks. "What? Why? We've been planning this for over a week."

"I know, I know," she says, her voice tinged with regret. "But it's important. I'm really sorry. Can we reschedule?"

I grip the phone tighter, frustration bubbling up. "It needs to be the new moon. I'll figure a ride out." I try not to sound cold; she has been nothing but supportive.

"No! Don't," she sounds frustrated. "We'll do it on the 31st. That's the next new moon. I won't bail again, I promise."

"I don't know, Tay—it's an entire month. What if I chicken out?"

"Don't... Please?" She sounds like she is about to cry. I don't know why it's so important she be the one—but I hate disappointing her.

"Fine," I say. "The 31st it is. But if you bail again, I'll take an Uber."

"Thank you, thank you, thank you!" she squeals.

I hang up, staring at the phone. Reschedule. Great. Just when I thought everything was coming together. I don't know if I can wait another full month, but I am going to have to.

I wonder why she had to cancel. Taylor doesn't talk about her home life much. Would it have been rude to ask? I open my laptop. Luke would be awake by now.

DreamSeeker: "Hey, my Lake 40 thing got canceled."

ArdentElan: "I'm so sorry. What happened?"

DreamSeeker: "My friend bailed last minute."

He didn't answer right away, so I made myself a cup of coffee. As I was stirring in some sugar, my phone buzzed.

ArdentElan: "I'm sure she had a good reason…"

I frowned at the screen. How does he know that?

DreamSeeker: "Yeah, she is. But it's still frustrating. I was really looking forward to it."

ArdentElan: "I know. You've been preparing so meticulously. Remember to keep an eye out for the moss-covered rock with the crack, past the 1.3-mile marker. That's where you place your personal item."

I felt a chill run down my spine. I hadn't mentioned that part to him yet.

DreamSeeker: "How did you know I was worried about finding the rock?"

There was a long pause before he replied.

ArdentElan: "I… looked up the ritual. Thought it might help if we both knew the steps."

I stared at his message, a sense of unease creeping over me. He was always so supportive, but sometimes he seemed to know too much.

DreamSeeker: "It's just... strange. Sometimes I feel like you know what I'm thinking."

ArdentElan: "Maybe I do. I care about you, and I pay attention. Like when you mentioned feeling watched during your rituals. That shadow you saw behind you... don't let it scare you too much. It's just part of the process."

My breath caught. Did I tell him about the shadow?

DreamSeeker: "Luke, how do you know about the shadow?"

There was another long pause.

ArdentElan: "I've experienced similar things. Sometimes, when you're connected, you can sense what others are going through. It's like we're on the same wavelength."

DreamSeeker: "That's...kind of nice."

More like creepy.

ArdentElan: "Just be careful. The Lake 40 Challenge is powerful. More powerful than you realize. Maybe we should practice more lucid dreaming. We could meet again, try to learn more in that state."

I put down my coffee cup, my hands trembling. This was all becoming too intense.

DreamSeeker: "I will. Thanks, Luke. I guess we'll see what happens."

ArdentElan: "I'll be at the Space Needle tonight. Hope to see you. And remember, I'm always here if you need to talk."

I closed the chat window; the unease lingering. How did he know so much? Was he just that intuitive, or was there something more to his knowledge? The line between my reality and the paranormal felt like it was blurring more with every interaction.

I decide to spend the day catching up on homework, but every small sound and movement catches my attention, making me feel a constant sense of being watched. The sky has turned a dull gray, the air thick with humidity. Every breath feels like pulling in a storm. I can't shake the feeling that something is off, as if the world itself is waiting for the worst to happen.

When I try to focus, but paranoia sets in. I see shapes in the corners of my eyes, hearing whispers when no one is around. Each time I turn to look, there's nothing there, but the feeling of being watched grows stronger. It's as though I am in between worlds. Once I complete the Lake 40 Challenge and enter the Fade for real, I will know the difference. There will be no more in-between.

As evening falls, I bail on the homework and decide to write a detailed journal entry instead, listing out the ritual steps again:

"Start at midnight, alone. Don't look back. Ignore the voices. Offer a personal item..."

I'm going to use my grandfather's old pocket watch. The act of writing calms me a little, but the sense of impending doom lingers. I should just get some sleep.

Just as I'm about to drift into a restless sleep, I hear a tapping at the window. My heart leaps into my throat. I turn to look, but there's nothing there. I think about turning on the lights, but I grab my phone and see a Discord message from Luke.

ArdentElan: "Don't forget. I'll be at the Space Needle tonight. Hope to see you."

I set my phone down, the message only adding to my anxiety. How did he know so much? Was he just that intuitive, or was there something more to his knowledge?

As I finally close my eyes, I can't shake the feeling that I'm not alone. The night seems to watch and wait, just like me.

CHAPTER 17

October 22, 2019

Dom pulled up to the row of homes on Maple Street as the sun dipped low, casting long, eerie shadows across the quiet neighborhood. The house he stopped in front of was unremarkable, with beige siding and a modest porch.

As he approached, he noticed the door was ajar. A chill ran down his spine, a sense of déjà vu transporting him back to New Orleans. He could almost smell the decay from those ritualistic murders, the heavy scent of death lingering in the humid air. Shaking off the memory, he focused on the present.

"Amanda?" he called out, his voice breaking the uneasy silence. "Amanda Weiss?" No answer. The faint sound of a television drifted from inside, mingling with the lingering aroma of incense. He could hear the narrator of *Ancient Aliens* droning on about extraterrestrial influences on human history.

His instincts took over, and he pushed the door open further. "Amanda Weiss?" he called again, stepping inside. The room was dim, shadows pooling in corners, adding to the unsettling atmosphere.

The living room was in disarray, as if someone had left in a hurry. An open bottle of Southern Comfort sat on the coffee table, its contents half-gone, and a glass next to it suggested someone had been drinking. The flickering TV cast an eerie glow on the walls, highlighting the curling tendrils of smoke from a burning stick of incense.

Dom's eyes swept the room. The air felt thick with unease, the kind of tension that made his skin crawl. He moved deeper into the house, the creak of the floorboards under his feet echoing through the space.

"Amanda!" he called again, louder this time. The only response was the background hum of the TV and the occasional creak of the old wooden floors settling.

His hand hovered near his holster as he advanced down the hallway, peering into rooms as he passed. Each was empty of people, yet filled with an unsettling stillness. Clothes were strewn on the floor of the bedroom, and the bathroom light flickered.

After turning a corner, Dom collided with a figure. "Ah!" he shouted, just as the woman screamed. They stumbled back, and she swung her arm, striking him across the chest.

"What are you doing in my house?" she yelled, her voice tinged with panic. Her eyes were wild, and her breath reeked of alcohol. She looked ready to strike again.

Dom raised his hands. "I'm with the police," he blurted, his voice calm but firm. "Can I show you my badge?"

Amanda hesitated, her breathing heavy. She yanked off her noise-canceling headset. "What did you say?"

"I am a police officer," he repeated. "I am going to show you my badge."

"You don't have a warrant," she snapped, her eyes narrowing.

"I can leave," Dom said, keeping his hands visible and his tone steady. "The door was open. I thought something had happened."

Amanda's gaze darted around the room, as if piecing together the situation. "Why are you here?" she asked, her voice softer now, but still wary.

"I have some questions about the Children of the Veil," Dom said, watching her reaction.

Her face went pale, and she shook her head, mumbling to herself. "This shit follows me everywhere." She let out a resigned sigh. "May as well have a seat," she muttered, gesturing to the cluttered living room.

Dom sat on the edge of the couch, noting Amanda's unfocused eyes and the faint smell of alcohol mingled with something more pungent. She slumped into an armchair opposite him, her movements sluggish and uncoordinated.

"Amanda, I need to ask you about the Children of the Veil," Dom began, keeping his tone calm and measured. "What can you tell me about the group and Malcolm Mitchell?"

"He is dead." Amanda's eyes flickered with a mixture of fear and irritation. She took a swig from the glass on the table, grimacing at the taste. "I left before that. When things got crazy," she said, her voice slurred. "Malcolm... he was obsessed, you know? Thought he could find..." Her voice trailed off.

Dom nodded, encouraging her to continue. "You said you left before Malcolm died. What happened that made you decide to leave?"

Amanda sighed, her eyes drifting to the TV where *Ancient Aliens* continued to play. "It just got too weird. Malcolm started talking about contacting... things from beyond. He was convinced he could unlock some... I was all for connecting with the other side, but what he wanted to do... I couldn't handle it. I was scared."

"What did he want to do?" Dom asked.

Amanda shook her head. "Nothing good, and that's all I'm gonna say about that."

Dom pressed. "Did Malcolm ever mention using children in his rituals?"

Amanda's eyes widened, and she took a deep breath. "Yeah, he did. He wanted to use my kid once. Said something about how the spirits favored the young and pure. I got the hell out of there after that."

She reached for a nearby photo album and flipped it open to a picture of a young boy. "This is my son, Daniel. He's an adult now, but we're estranged. Haven't spoken in years."

Dom studied the photo, a chill running down his spine. "I'm sorry to hear that. Did Malcolm refer to the spirits he wanted to contact by any specific name?"

"He called them 'Elan.' Said they were ancient beings waiting on the other side, in the Fade. He believed they held the key to unlimited power and knowledge." Dom made a mental note to look up the word "Ardent" later—he rarely heard "Elan" regarding spirits and wanted to understand Luke's connection to this term.

Dom leaned forward. "Do you know anything about what might have happened to Taylor after her dad passed away? Or if she is still connected to the Children of the Veil?"

Amanda shrugged, her eyes now wary. "I don't know. I haven't seen her in ages. After Malcolm died, I cut ties with everyone. Just wanted to forget it all."

"Have you heard anything about Lake 40?" Dom asked, watching her reaction.

Amanda's face twitched, a shadow of fear passing over her features. "Lake 40… that place is bad news. Malcolm always talked about it being some kind of gateway. It had history, ya know. Said he could feel something there."

Dom sensed her reluctance. "Do you have any idea what Malcolm was trying to achieve? What his goal was?"

Amanda hesitated, her gaze dropping to her lap. "I… I don't know the details. He kept a lot to himself, especially toward the end. I just know he was desperate, convinced he was on the verge of some big discovery."

Dom sighed. This was getting them nowhere fast, and he didn't want to push too hard in case he needed her later. "If you think of anything else, anything at all that might help, please let me know."

Amanda nodded, taking another drink. "Yeah, sure."

Dom stood up and handed her his card. "Thank you for your time, Amanda. I'll let myself out."

She was already passed out.

As he walked back to the door, the oppressive feeling of the house seemed to lift, but the sense of unease lingered. Amanda's information was sparse, but it confirmed his suspicions that the cult's influence ran deep and that Taylor was likely caught in its dark web.

As Dom stepped outside, the cool evening air providing a welcome respite from the oppressive atmosphere of Amanda's home, he heard her voice calling from the door.

"Hey, wait! Here, you can have this," Amanda said, her words slurred. She held out a worn pamphlet, its pages yellowed with age.

Dom turned and walked back towards her, taking the pamphlet from her outstretched hand. "What is it?"

"It's got the challenge marked," she said, her eyes glassy but serious. "Might help you understand what Malcolm was so obsessed with."

The pamphlet she handed him was old, the date on the front long since faded. It looked like some kind of farmer's almanac; the cover illustrated with pastoral scenes and arcane symbols. The page caught Dom's attention.

"Thanks, Amanda," Dom said, pocketing the pamphlet. "Get some rest."

As he walked back to his car, he couldn't resist skimming through the pages. There were handwritten instructions that made his blood run cold. This was the Lake 40 Challenge. The ink was faded and the paper brittle, but the details were unmistakable. The pamphlet had to be at least 100 years old.

He sat in his car under the dim streetlight and read the instructions. The challenge outlined a midnight hike to Lake 40, performed on a moonless night. Participants were instructed to walk without looking back, leave a personal item on a moss-covered rock, and sit by the lake listening for a baby's cry. If successful, they would see a dark figure in the water, but were warned to avoid eye contact.

Dom felt a chill as he realized the ritual described in this ancient pamphlet matched the one Lily had written about in her journal. The instructions were precise, hinting at an age-old practice that had persisted through the centuries.

This pamphlet was a link to the past, to the dark history of the Children of the Veil and their leader, Malcolm Mitchell. It suggested a continuity of belief and practice that spanned generations. Dom knew he needed to show this to Lauren.

Dom climbed into his car, the feeling from Amanda's home still lingering. He pulled out his phone and called Lauren.

She answered on the second ring. "Dom, what's up?"

"Did you have any luck with Richard Hale?" he asked, starting the engine and pulling away from the curb.

"No, he wouldn't talk," Lauren replied, frustration clear in her voice. "Asked for a lawyer almost immediately. It was a dead end."

Dom sighed, gripping the steering wheel tighter. "I had a bit more luck with Amanda Weiss. She was pretty out of it, probably drunk and maybe high, but she gave me something interesting. An old pamphlet looks like some kind of farmer's almanac. It's ancient, but the page she b ookmarked... it's the Lake 40 Challenge. The instructions match what Lily wrote in her journal."

"Really?" Lauren sounded intrigued. "What does it say?"

"It's detailed," Dom replied, glancing at the pamphlet on the passenger seat. "Same stuff as in Lily's journal, but it has to be at least 100 years old. It ties directly to what Malcolm Mitchell was doing."

There was a moment of silence on the line as Lauren processed this information. "We need to check this out ourselves," she finally said. "Tomorrow, we should make the hike and visit all the spots mentioned in the pamphlet and the journal."

Dom felt a pang of dread at the thought of hiking. He wasn't a fan of the outdoors—the bugs, the unpredictability. Worse, it made him think about his nightmare—running through the woods, pursued by an unseen terror.

"Agreed. We need to see if there's anything tangible at these locations. Maybe we'll find some clues that can help us understand what happened to Lily and what the cult is really after."

"Alright," Lauren said. "I'll pick you up early tomorrow. Bring the pamphlet and anything else you think might be useful. Get ready for a hike."

"I'll see you then," Dom replied. "And Lauren... be careful tonight. Something about this feels... off."

"You too, Dom," she breathed. "See you tomorrow."

As Dom hung up and pocketed his phone, he glanced in the rearview mirror. The dim light from the streetlamp cast eerie shadows inside the car. His reflection stared back at him, weary and troubled. He closed his eyes for a moment, trying to center himself.

When he opened them, he gasped. Lily's face was in the mirror, her eyes wide with fear. She mouthed something, but no sound came through.

Her image flickered, as if struggling to maintain contact. Her eyes darted to the side, and Dom could almost feel her panic.

"Lily?" he whispered, his voice trembling. "What are you trying to tell me?"

Her expression grew more desperate, her mouth forming silent words. Dom focused, straining to understand.

"Don't..." she mouthed, but her image wavered, the connection weakening, and the words were lost.

Chapter 18

July 1, 2019

I checked the lunar calendar. Since Taylor bailed tomorrow, the next one is August 1st. It's a Thursday, so I requested both days off from work. I will go to school in the morning, then Taylor will come over and take me to the trailhead that night (assuming she doesn't bail again). She swears she's in it, so all I can do is trust her. I don't want to admit it, but she is probably right about doing it next month. Camping is super popular the week of the 4th, and I don't need some drunk person showing up and ruining my ritual.

Last night, I decided not to practice my lucid dreaming. Something about Luke had set me off, and I needed to process it. Despite this, I still ended up on top of the Space Needle. I don't know if it was a regular dream or lucid. I was on the observation deck, and it was so dark. The moon was a fraction of a sliver—it made sense because tonight was the actual new moon.

I started walking around the deck, looking out over the city. A part of me wondered if I would run into Luke (being unsure what was real). So I just kept walking. The cityscape kept changing, morphing into something alien and endless. After some time, I glimpsed a shadow. This had to be Luke. I started walking faster, and so did it. Then I was running, chasing it. It went faster too. Before long, it had progressed so far ahead; it was chasing me.

My stomach felt cold, and all I knew was I had to get away. Then I remembered I had been chasing it.

So I stopped to face it.

Luke was there, in jeans and a dark hoodie that covered his face. I approached and pushed back the hood. But it wasn't Luke's face—it was my own. But instead of eyes, all I could see were black, empty holes.

When I attempted to scream, my voice refused to come. The silence was stifling, an almost physical force pressing down on me. The void where my eyes should have been consumed the light, drawing me into its depths. I was pulled closer; the darkness encircling me like a suffocating veil.

The world around me dissolved, the deck of the Space Needle fading into an abyss. The city below twisted and warped, buildings bending at impossible angles, stretching into the sky like skeletal fingers. Shadows slithered across the ground, merging and shifting, whispering my name in a cacophony of voices.

I tried to run, but my legs felt like they were encased in concrete. Each step was a struggle, a battle against an unseen force pulling me back. The figure—my figure—stood still, watching me with those empty, soulless eyes. I could feel its gaze piercing through me, an icy chill that seeped into my bones.

Desperation clawed at me as I reached out, trying to grasp something, anything, to anchor myself. My hand passed through the railing as if it were smoke, and I stumbled forward, teetering on the edge. Below me, the cityscape had transformed into a swirling vortex of darkness, a bottomless pit that seemed to pulse with malevolent intent.

The ground beneath my feet crumbled away, sending me tumbling into the abyss. Wind filled my ears as shadows reached up, wrapping around me, pulling me deeper into the void. Just before everything went black, my face appeared, grinning with empty eyes.

And then, there was nothing but the darkness.

Suffice to say, I didn't sleep the rest of the night.

Today, I decide it's a good day to skip the Fade ritual. I have Intro to Astronomy, and I'm getting more into this class, especially after spending so much time reading up on the lunar calendar. We're preparing a lab to observe the phases of the Moon this month. I even get there early.

My partner's name is Ava. She is quiet like me, but I can tell she is excited. Our objective is to observe and record the phases of the Moon over a month, analyze the data, and understand the relationship between the Moon's phases and its position relative to the Earth and the Sun. This lab will be part of our final. The teacher gives us time to discuss and divide the work.

"I'm actually going to be doing a night hike on the next new moon," I say. "I can get some pictures for documentation."

Ava's eyes brighten. "So cool! Are you going to be out of the city? I wonder if you can actually capture something!"

"I read that it's next to impossible, unless it's during an eclipse, but I want to try!"

"Night hiking sounds scary. Are you doing it to look at the stars? Do you have a telescope?" Her words come out in a rush.

"No," I laugh, then feel my face heat. "It's actually for a paranormal ritual thing," I confess, feeling unusually bold today. "Kind of like the Elevator Game."

"Oh! I've heard of the Elevator Game. That's terrifying. You are so brave."

"Stupid probably," I giggle. "But I have to know and see if I can actually get to the Fade."

"I can't wait to hear about it."

"I'm taking notes too," I share. "Trying to follow a scientific method to a point. Like journaling, mostly."

"Smart," Ava replies.

Her enthusiasm is contagious, and for the first time in a while, I feel a genuine thrill at the prospect of sharing my experiences. Maybe this partnership will be more than just a project.

CHAPTER 19

October 23, 2019

Lauren arrived with the sun, coffee in hand. After a 45-minute drive, the Mountain Loop Highway unfolded in its seasonal splendor. Vibrant leaves almost rivaled those of New England, though not quite. Crisp autumn air, fragrant with pine and earth, provided a welcome break from the city's smog. Twisting through the mountains, the road revealed a landscape painted in red, orange, and gold, with each turn offering a more breathtaking view than the last.

Dom stepped out of the car. He was not a fan of hiking but unable to deny the stunning scenery. The fresh air invigorated him despite his reluctance, and he had to admit, it was gorgeous out here.

Lauren followed, taking a deep breath. She radiated energy, her eyes sparkling with the thrill of adventure. The mountains stood in the distance, their hidden paths and secrets beckoning them to explore.

"What's got you so chipper this morning?" Dom asked. He was leaning against his car, arms crossed, looking as if he'd rather be anywhere else.

See handed him a protein bar. "I love to hike, and I love work. Who would have thought I could ever put the two of them together?" she replied, giving Dom a playful wink.

Dom sighed, accepting the snack. He preferred to break a sweat somewhere with more immediate amenities. The small-town attitude and the stares directed at anyone who looked different only added to his discomfort. Lauren understood this, and they agreed to avoid the nearby town.

He glanced at Lauren, who was adjusting her backpack and checking her gear with practiced efficiency. Her enthusiasm was contagious, but Dom couldn't shake the unease that had settled in his chest. He pulled out the photocopy of the pamphlet and read aloud, "Start your hike at the Lake 40 Trailhead at midnight on a moonless night. Be alone. If there's people around, do not proceed."

"Well, we already failed at that one," Lauren giggled. "It's not night or moonless, and I would guess having two of us does not constitute being alone." Her laughter was light, cutting through Dom's dark mood, but it did little to ease his apprehension.

Before they started up the trail, Dom looked around the scene from last week. You would have never guessed anything had happened. The combination of the crime lab and wilderness had erased any evidence of the horror. Nature had a way of swallowing secrets, its calm facade hiding the darkness that lurked beneath.

As they stood at the edge of the trail, Dom took a deep breath, trying to center himself. The forest stretched out before them, a maze of trees and undergrowth that seemed to close in around the narrow path. The air was cool and crisp, a contrast to the tension coiling in his stomach.

"Beautiful, isn't it?" Lauren said, breaking the silence. She was looking out at the trail.

"Yeah, it is," Dom replied, though his voice lacked conviction. His eyes darted to the shadows between the trees, half-expecting to see the figure from his nightmares materialize. He forced himself to focus on the path ahead, on the task at hand. They were here to find answers.

Lauren gave him a reassuring smile. "You'll be fine, Dom. Just think of it as another case. We follow the clues, and we'll sort this out."

Dom appreciated her attempt to ease his mind. "Yeah, just another case," he muttered, though he knew this one was different. Then he read the next step. "Walk steadily and don't look back. If you hear noises or voices behind you, ignore them."

"Let's get going," Lauren said.

Dom took one last look at the parking lot, then turned to follow Lauren. There was no turning back now.

The next mile of hiking was uneventful. The hardest part was resisting the urge to look back. Lauren, intent on following the instructions, expected nothing supernatural to happen. Dom, however, was not so sure. Every snap of a twig and every bird call set him on edge as they trudged forward. The trail was gaining elevation, and Dom could feel sweat breaking out on his brow.

They noted the mile markers as they passed them. At the 1-mile mark, Dom pulled out the photocopy of the pamphlet and read aloud, "Shortly after a mile, find a moss-covered rock with a crack. Put a personal item inside. Stay focused on the rock and trail."

Lauren kept her eyes forward. "Lily's journal mentioned it being just after the 1.3-mile marker. We need to be on the lookout for that."

It wasn't long after that they found the rock. The gash in its surface looked like a wound, raw and gaping, revealing trinkets and coins nestled deep inside. Dom peered closer, wondering if so many people had really attempted the ritual, or if this rock had become some sort of makeshift wishing well.

"Did you bring a personal item?" he asked Lauren.

She pulled out a small silver pendant, its delicate chain glinting in the dappled sunlight. Then she tossed it into the crack, where it settled out of sight. Turning to Dom, her expression serious, she said, "We should both put something in, just in case."

Dom sighed. He had been hoping to avoid this. Personal items held significance and, in the world he knew, could give someone—or something—power over you. He reached into his pocket and pulled out a smooth rock. He placed it into the crack.

"A little piece of home," he explained when he noticed Lauren's questioning look.

He collected rocks from wherever he went, each one a tangible memory of a place and time. He had plenty from New Orleans and could bear to part with one. As the rock slipped into the crevice, Dom felt a subtle shift in the atmosphere, as if the forest itself acknowledged their offerings. The air grew cooler, and the shadows seemed to deepen.

The hike grew more challenging, with parts where they needed to scramble up rocks. Dom grumbled, "Who puts a lake at the top of a mountain, anyway?"

Lauren chuckled, her voice echoing off the trees. "Just think of it as an adventure."

Dom shook his head but couldn't suppress a smile. They pressed on; the trail becoming steeper and more treacherous. Loose stones slid under their feet, and they had to use their hands to steady themselves as they climbed.

"At the lake, sit facing the water. Close your eyes and listen. If you don't hear a baby's cry, the ritual failed," Dom read aloud from the pamphlet during a brief pause to catch his breath.

"We have a ways to go before we reach the lake," Lauren commented, starting back up the trail.

Dom followed, his muscles protesting with each step. As they gained elevation, the air grew thinner, and the temperature dropped. Vibrant colors of the leaves faded into a more muted palette of evergreen and rocky outcroppings. The forest grew sparser, with the canopy above allowing more sunlight to filter through.

They scrambled over a large boulder, and Dom stopped, looking around at the imposing trees that seemed to watch their every move. The sense of unease that had been gnawing at him since the start of the hike intensified.

"How much further?" Dom asked, trying to keep the strain out of his voice.

"Not far now," Lauren replied, her tone light but her eyes betraying her own weariness. "We should be there soon."

Dom wiped the sweat from his brow. As they pushed forward, the trail leveled out. The trees thinned further, and a glimmer of water appeared through the foliage. The sight of the lake brought a mix of relief and apprehension. They had reached their destination.

The lake was a mirror of stillness, its surface reflecting the sky above. The surrounding trees stood like silent sentinels, their reflections creating an illusion of depth.

Lauren approached the edge of the water, her steps slow and deliberate. "This is it," she said, her voice a whisper. "Are you ready?"

They sat down facing the water, the pamphlet's instructions fresh in their minds. Dom closed his eyes and listened. Minutes stretched into an eternity. The only sounds were the occasional rustle of leaves and the distant call of a bird. His heart pounded in his chest, each beat echoing in his ears.

A faint cry pierced the silence, like the wail of a distant baby. Dom's eyes snapped open, meeting Lauren's wide-eyed gaze. They had both heard it.

"That had to have been a bird," Lauren whispered, her voice tinged with uncertainty.

Dom was not so sure. His voice was very quiet as he read, "If you hear the cry, look into the water. Keep your gaze steady even if you see shapes or hear whispers."

He gazed into the water, seeing the sky and mountains reflecting back at him. But more than that, he saw the outline of a young woman staring at him. He reached a hand out as she reached back at him, their fingers stretching toward each other. The trance deepened, and Dom leaned further and further until he almost lost his balance and fell in.

Lauren's hand pulling him back snapped him out of whatever spell he was under. She was laughing. "Dom, did you fall asleep?"

He shook his head and blinked, the eerie vision still vivid in his mind. "You didn't see that?"

Lauren looked confused. "See what?"

"I swear I saw Lily Chen," Dom said, his voice trembling.

"I think you were dreaming. I am pretty sure you fell asleep. Read the next part."

Dom pulled out the paper, trying to steady his shaking hands. "If a dark figure appears, you've succeeded. Avoid its eyes and don't answer its questions." He continued with the last two steps. "Regardless of the result, leave without looking back or taking your item. Following these steps will grant you special sight, revealing hidden paths. Never share your experience. Speaking of it attracts unwelcome attention from the Fade."

The words hung in the air, a chilling reminder of the danger they were courting. The lake's surface rippled, distorting the reflections. Dom couldn't shake the feeling of being watched, the oppressive atmosphere pressing in on him.

An icy wind blew through the trees, sending a shiver down Dom's spine. The silence was deafening, broken only by the faint, eerie whisper of the wind. He glanced back at the water and froze. A dark figure emerged in the lake, its outline growing clearer with each second, exuding an unsettling presence.

"Do you see that?" he whispered, his voice trembling.

Lauren's eyes widened in fear. "I thought this only worked on a moonless night."

The figure pulsed, its form shifting and flickering. Dom's heart pounded in his chest, the oppressive dread overwhelming him.

"We need to go," he said, his voice barely above a whisper. "Now."

Lauren's earlier bravado gone. They stood up, careful not to look back at the water. The sense of urgency was overwhelming as they started down the trail, their footsteps quickening with each step.

The forest seemed to close in around them; the shadows deepening with every passing moment. Dom felt an unshakeable presence behind them, a silent observer just out of sight. He resisted the urge to turn around, knowing that breaking the rules could have dire consequences. The path ahead seemed longer and more treacherous, the air thick with foreboding. This was too much like his dream for comfort.

They reached the trailhead without incident, but the sense of unease lingered. Dom glanced at Lauren, her face pale and drawn. Whatever they had encountered at Lake 40 had left a mark on both of them.

"Let's get out of here," Lauren whispered, eyes still wide with fear.

Dom nodded in agreement. They wasted no time getting into the car. Dom started the engine, and they sped away, the dark memories receding in the rearview mirror.

The drive down Mountain Loop Highway was silent. After what felt like an eternity, they reached a small diner on the outskirts of Lake Stevens. The bright lights and the hum of activity were comforting. Dom parked the car, and they both sat there for a moment, gathering their thoughts.

"We need to talk about this," Dom said, breaking the silence. "But not here. Let's grab something to eat inside and find a quiet corner."

Lauren was still shaken. They entered the diner, the warmth and bustle of the place a welcome respite. They found a booth in the back, away from prying ears, and ordered lunch.

Dom took a deep breath, his hands still trembling. "What do you think we saw back there?"

Lauren sipped her coffee, her eyes distant. "I don't know, but it felt real. Now I wonder if it could have just been a shadow."

Dom leaned forward, lowering his voice. "The Children of the Veil. This has to be connected. The ritual, the dark figure, it all ties back to them. Remember what Amanda said about Malcolm Mitchell and his obsession with Lake 40? This has to be part of what he was trying to uncover."

"And the pamphlet Amanda gave us mentioned rituals that grant special sight. If people have been performing these rituals for generations, they might have a better understanding of what we experienced."

Dom pulled out his notebook, flipping through the pages. "Malcolm Mitchell believed Lake 40 was a gateway. If the Children of the Veil were trying to access something through these rituals, it could explain why they were so desperate to keep it secret. We need to find out more about their practices, their history. And, what does it have to do with Lily Chen?"

Lauren tapped her finger on the table, lost in thought. "We should also see if we can get Taylor to talk to us again. She might know more than she realizes."

"She's been through a lot, but we need to approach her carefully. She's already terrified."

Lauren leaned in. "And what about the others who left the cult? Like Amanda. There must be more people out there who know something, even if they don't realize it, or perhaps they know what happened to Lily, or even worse, part of it. We should track others down and try to talk to Amanda again, too. See if they can provide any insights."

Dom scribbled down notes, their task settling over him like a shroud. "Agreed. We should also look into any other missing persons or unexplained deaths around here. There might be a trail of victims we haven't connected yet."

The waitress brought over a fresh pot of coffee, and they paused their conversation until she left.

Dom hesitated for a moment before speaking. "Lauren, there's something else. I've been seeing Lily. Not just in dreams, but in mirrors, at odd times. It's like she's trying to tell me something."

Lauren's eyes widened. "Why didn't you tell me sooner?"

Dom sighed. "I thought it was stress, or maybe I was losing it. But after what we saw at the lake, I think she's connected to all of this. Maybe she's trying to guide us."

Before Lauren could respond, Dom's phone buzzed on the table. He glanced at the screen, seeing a message from Detective Collins.

"What's up?" Lauren asked, noticing Dom's expression change.

Dom opened the message and read aloud, "Get to the station. Now."

Lauren blinked. "What do you think it is?"

Dom shook his head, already reaching for his coat. "I don't know, but it sounds important."

They settled their bill and rushed out of the diner, their unfinished conversation and uneaten lunch left behind. The drive to the station was tense, each lost in their thoughts about what awaited them. Dom's phone buzzed again. Another message from Collins, this one even more urgent: "We traced 'ArdentElan's' IP address. We're preparing a warrant."

Lauren's eyes widened with shock.

Dom's jaw tightened. "Let's get inside and find out what Collins has uncovered."

Chapter 20

July 10, 2019

It's been an amazing couple of weeks. Last Sunday, I did the Lake 40 hike again. The trail was pretty crowded this time. I took my friend Ava from school. I invited Taylor too, but she was weird about it—jealous, I think—and cryptic about why she couldn't come. Ava asked me a couple of questions about the Lake 40 Challenge, but mostly, it was just for fun. I've never had a lot of friends, so it was a little overwhelming, especially having an envious friend.

We located the 1.3-mile marker and found the moss-covered rock with a prominent crack. It's going to be hard to find at night, so I noted the surrounding trees. Even during the day, the place felt heavy. Regardless, I'm feeling more prepared.

Today, we have lab prep, and Ava is already at our table when I arrive in the classroom.

"I can't believe how clear the moon was last night!" Ava says, her eyes shining.

"Waxing gibbous," I giggle, feeling like an expert. "Did you get a picture for the presentation?"

"I did!" she replies, pulling out her phone to show me. Ava is a brilliant photographer.

"That's pretty incredible," I tell her, admiring the shot.

"Hey!" she blurts. "Wanna get lunch after class?"

"Sure!" I agree, then remember, "Oh... I forgot. I'm supposed to meet Taylor."

"It's okay," Ava says, but her face falls a little.

"No—why don't you come with me? I'm just supposed to meet a friend at Starbucks."

Ava shrugs and smiles. "Sure, why not! As long as I'm not intruding on anything."

"You're not," I assure her, feeling a bit more at ease. "Taylor will be happy to see you." I'm not sure how accurate that is.

Ava and I walk in, the familiar smell of coffee and baked goods wrapping around us like a warm blanket. I spot Taylor sitting by the window with a book open in front of her. She looks up as we approach, her expression shifting when she sees Ava with me. It's subtle, but there—a flicker of something in her eyes that's gone almost as quickly as it appears.

"Hey, Taylor!" I greet, sliding into the seat across from her. "This is my friend, Ava. She's in my astronomy class."

Taylor smiles, but it doesn't quite reach her eyes. "Hi, Ava. Nice to meet you." Her voice is warm enough, but there's an undercurrent I can't quite place.

"Nice to meet you too, Taylor," Ava says, setting her bag down. "Lily talks about you all the time."

Taylor's smile tightens. "All good things, I hope."

"Of course," Ava replies, oblivious to the slight tension. "We just came from class. We're working on a presentation about the moon phases."

"Sounds interesting," Taylor says, closing her book and setting it aside. "Lily mentioned you were into photography. Have any good shots?"

Ava beams, pulling out her phone. "I got a great one of the waxing gibbous last night. Here, look."

Taylor leans forward, her eyes flicking to the screen. "Nice. You've got a good eye."

"Thanks!" Ava says, pleased. "We're using it for our presentation. The details are just amazing."

Taylor nods, but her gaze shifts back to me. "So, Lily, what have you been up to?"

I hesitate, feeling a bit of the awkwardness between them. "Just busy with school and stuff. Ava and I did the Lake 40 hike again last Sunday."

"Yeah, Lily mentioned the challenge," Ava adds. "That Lake 40 Challenge thing sounds intense. Have you ever done it?"

Taylor's expression flickers again. "No, I haven't. It's more Lily's thing. I'm more of a... spectator, I guess."

Ava nods, not seeming to catch the slight edge in Taylor's tone. "Well, it was a fun hike. We should all go together sometime."

Taylor's smile returns, but it feels more like a mask. "Maybe. I've been pretty busy lately."

There's a brief, awkward silence before Ava breaks it. "So, what are you reading?" she asks, gesturing to the book.

I see the title, *Adult Children of Emotionally Immature Parents.*

Taylor glances at Ava, then places the book face down on the table. "Oh, just some light fiction."

I say nothing. From what I know, both of Taylor's parents are dead. Maybe it's for a class.

"That's cool," Ava says, looking genuine.

As they chat, I can't shake the feeling that something is off. Taylor's reactions are too measured, her smile a touch too forced. I make a mental note to talk to her later, hoping to smooth over whatever tension there is. For now, I focus on keeping the conversation flowing, trying to bridge the gap between my two friends.

When I head home after what feels like an endless day, I'm still unsettled. The walk back to my apartment is filled with thoughts swirling in my mind, making me eager for a familiar, comforting distraction. Once inside, I drop my bag and take a deep breath, trying to shake off the day. Reaching out to Luke gives me a sense of relief.

DreamSeeker: Hey! You there?

The screen blinks a moment later with his response.

ArdentElan: Hey! How's it going?

DreamSeeker: It's been an interesting day. I took my friend Ava to the Lake 40 trail for another dry run. I think I found the exact spot to put my item. The place is so strange, even in daylight.

ArdentElan: That's great! Well, not the strange part, but finding the spot. Did you make notes or take pictures to help you remember?

DreamSeeker: Yeah, I noted the trees around it and took a few pictures. The entire area feels... heavy, you know?

ArdentElan: That's the magic of places like that. They have a presence. It's natural to feel that way. The important thing is to stay calm and focused during the challenge. The atmosphere can get to you if you let it.

DreamSeeker: Thanks. I'll try to remember that. Any other tips for staying calm?

ArdentElan: Breathing exercises help. Also, keep a goal in mind. Remember why you're doing this. And if things get too intense, it's okay to take a step back and regroup.

I lean back in my chair, feeling a bit more at ease. Luke always has a way of making everything seem manageable. Our conversations have been more frequent and comforting this past week, and it feels good to have someone who understands and supports my obsession with the paranormal. The uncomfortable feeling from before is gone.

DreamSeeker: That's helpful. I've been feeling overwhelmed. Taylor's been acting weird, and I'm not sure why.

ArdentElan: Maybe she's just worried about you. This kind of stuff can be hard for people to understand. It's important to keep your friends close, but don't let their concerns deter you from your goals.

DreamSeeker: You're right. It's just... I've never been good with people, and having a jealous friend is unfamiliar territory for me.

ArdentElan: You've come this far. Just keep doing what you're doing, and things will fall into place.

I smile at the screen. Despite the oddities and unsettling moments, talking to Luke makes everything feel more normal. He's a constant, reliable presence in my life, someone who shares my interests and understands my passion for the unknown.

DreamSeeker: Thanks, Luke. I appreciate it. I'll keep you updated on everything.

ArdentElan: Anytime. I'm here for you. Just remember, stay calm and stay focused. You've got this.

As I close my laptop, I can't help but feel that things are falling into place. The whispers of doubt are still there, but they're quieter now, overshadowed by a growing sense of confidence.

CHAPTER 21

October 23, 2019

T he city blurred past the car windows as they sped through the streets. Dom's mind raced with thoughts of Lily, Taylor, and the Children of the Veil. When they pulled into the station, the building loomed against the blue sky. Dom felt a sense of foreboding as they entered. He led the way to Collins' office, his stride matched by Lauren's steps.

Collins looked up as they entered, his expression grave. "Dom, Lauren, you need to see this," he said, gesturing to the computer screen. "We've tracked down ArdentElan's IP address."

Dom leaned in, his eyes scanning the data displayed on the monitor. The screen showed a map with a highlighted area in Everett, WA, pinpointing a neighborhood along

Lowell Larimar Road. As he absorbed the information, an icy knot of dread settled in his stomach. The implications were staggering, the connections undeniable.

Lauren peered over his shoulder, her eyes widening as she took in the details. "Wait, I thought Luke said he was in Florida. But this IP address... it's local."

Collins nodded. "We confirmed it. The IP address is registered to an address on Lowell Larimar Road. It's linked to the old Children of the Veil Enclave property."

Dom's eyes narrowed. "That's Taylor's home. This... this changes everything."

Lauren gasped, her hand flying to her mouth. "Taylor's been right under our noses this whole time. We need to get there immediately."

Dom straightened, urgency propelling him into action. "If Luke is using Taylor's home, or if she's involved more than we thought, we can't afford to wait. We need to get a team together and head over there now."

"Let's move."

The afternoon sun cast a warm, golden light over the farmlands on the outskirts of Everett. Here, the city gave way to peaceful expanses of green, transforming into a different world. Barns and grazing cattle dotted the landscape, a contrast to the bustling neighborhoods and city areas just a mile away in each direction. The farmhouse, at the end of a long gravel driveway, exuded a tranquility that belied the tension simmering within. Dom adjusted his tactical gear, feeling the weight of the situation more than the equipment.

As the SWAT team moved with precision, their black uniforms stark against the lush greenery, Dom's mind raced. This case had been a labyrinth of dead ends and false leads. Now, standing before this unassuming farmhouse, he felt a flicker of hope and anxiety intertwine.

The team leader, a burly man with a stern expression, approached the front door and pounded a rhythmic knock that echoed in the still air. "SWAT team! Open up!"

Dom's pulse quickened as he scanned the surroundings, every rustle of leaves amplified in the quiet. The door creaked open, revealing Taylor, her face pale and eyes wide with fear. Dom felt a pang of empathy, but he pushed it aside, focusing on the task at hand.

Taylor stepped aside, allowing the team to enter. Dom followed, his eyes scanning the cozy living room, noting the mismatched furniture and the faint scent of lavender. Despite its warmth, a chill hung in the air, setting his nerves on edge.

Taylor was now perched on the edge of an armchair, her fingers fidgeting with the hem of her sweater. Dom studied her, noting the slight tremor in her hands and the way her gaze never settled on any of the team members. She was hiding something; he could feel it.

"We're here about the IP address connected to Arden-tElan's activities," the team leader stated, his voice cutting through the tension.

Taylor's voice trembled. "I... I don't know anything about it. I swear, I do not know how my IP address got involved."

Dom watched her, every hesitation, every nervous glance a potential clue. "Taylor, we need you to be honest with us. This is serious," he said, trying to keep his voice steady and reassuring.

Her breath hitched. "I'm telling you everything I know."

Dom exchanged a look with Lauren, who had noticed Taylor's furtive glances toward the hallway. "Is there someone else here, Taylor?" Dom asked, his tone softening, hoping to coax the truth out of her.

Taylor's eyes widened before she shook her head. "No, no one else. It's just me."

Dom's patience was wearing thin, but he knew pressing too hard could backfire. He softened his tone further. "If you know something, now is the time to tell us. Hiding information could be dangerous for you."

Her hands were clenched in her lap. "I'm telling you everything I know," she insisted, though Dom could hear the quiver in her voice. She was terrified, and it was clear she wasn't being truthful.

The team leader stepped forward, his expression hardening. "Taylor, if there's anything else you're not telling us..."

Dom watched as her eyes filled with tears. "I... I don't know how it happened. I just know that someone has been using my Wi-Fi. I didn't know it was for anything illegal, I swear!"

Dom felt a pang of sympathy. She seemed scared, but fear could drive people to desperate measures.

"Let's start here and move room by room," Dom said to Lauren, gesturing for a team member to stay with Taylor.

Lauren's keen eyes already scanning for anything out of place. They moved with practiced efficiency, checking behind furniture, inside closets, and under rugs. Dom could feel his pulse in his temples, a constant reminder of the high stakes.

As they entered the kitchen, the room was filled with the afternoon light; the warmth contrasting with the cold professionalism of their search. Dom opened cupboards and drawers, finding only the mundane items of daily life. His frustration grew with each passing second.

"Anything?" Lauren asked, her voice steady but edged with tension.

"Nothing yet," Dom replied, his tone mirroring her concern.

They moved to the dining room, its large wooden table standing like a silent witness to countless family meals.

Dom's mind wandered to the life Taylor must have led here before this nightmare began. The thoughts were pushed aside as he opened the china cabinet, finding only dishes and silverware.

Their search took them to a small study, cluttered with books and papers. Dom noted the variety of genres on the shelves, from thrillers to romance novels, and the different styles of handwriting in the scattered notes. Sifting through the desk, he hoped for a clue, a hint—anything. His frustration mounted as he found nothing of immediate interest.

Lauren stood by the window, looking out at the peaceful farmlands, a stark contrast to the tension inside. "We need to find something," she said, more to herself than to Dom.

"Let's check the upstairs next."

They moved to the staircase, each step creaking under their weight. Dom's senses were on high alert, every sound amplified in the quiet house. They reached the top and began their methodical search of the bedrooms.

In the first bedroom, Dom rifled through the drawers of a nightstand, finding only a few personal items. Lauren checked the closet, pushing aside clothes to look for any hidden compartments or unusual items. Again, they found nothing out of the ordinary.

The second bedroom was uneventful. Dom felt his frustration turn into a gnawing anxiety. Time was slipping away, and they needed to find something that could lead them closer to this ArdentElan.

As they entered the main bedroom, Dom paused. The room was neat, almost too neat. His eyes narrowed as he searched, going through each piece of furniture. Lauren joined him, her eyes scanning every corner.

Dom's attention was drawn to a small chest at the foot of the bed. He knelt down, his fingers tracing the edges of the lid. It seemed ordinary enough, but something felt off. With a careful motion, he opened it, revealing a collection of blankets and old family photos of a man, woman, and infant.

Lauren watched him, her eyes sharp. "Do you think that's Malcolm Mitchell with his wife and Taylor?"

Dom studied the images for a moment before shaking his head. "Could be. It would explain a lot."

"Anything else?"

"Not yet," Dom replied, feeling the weight of disappointment. "Let's keep looking. There has to be something here."

They moved to the attached bathroom, searching the cabinets and drawers.

As they finished their sweep bedroom, Dom felt unsettled. They had found nothing unusual so far, but his instincts told him there was more to discover. The serene landscape outside, with its deceptive calm, seemed to mock their efforts.

"We need to be thorough," Dom said, his voice resolute. "Let's check the basement."

They headed back downstairs. When they reached the basement door, they found it locked. Dom's heart skipped a beat, his instincts screaming that something significant lay beyond.

He turned to Taylor, who was hovering nearby. "Taylor, we need to get into the basement. Do you have the key?"

Taylor's eyes widened with fear, her hands trembling. "I-I don't have it," she stammered.

Dom's patience was thinning. "Taylor, if you don't have the key, we'll have to bust it down. Is that what you want?"

Taylor's resolve crumbled. She bit her lip, hesitating for a moment before producing a small tarnished key from her pocket. "Okay, I'll unlock it."

Dom watched her as she fumbled with the lock, hearing the click as the door creaked open. The basement stairs descended into darkness.

Dom and Lauren exchanged a glance. Their senses were heightened as they made their way down the steps. The basement was dimly lit, the air cooler and filled with a faint, musty odor. The hum of computer equipment broke the silence, drawing their attention.

Rows of servers and monitors lined the walls, casting a blue glow across the concrete floor. Dom's pulse quickened. This was it—this was what they had been looking for. They spread out, examining the setup, noting the so-phisticated nature of the equipment.

"Check every corner," Dom instructed, his voice a low whisper. Lauren moved toward the far end of the room.

As Dom approached the water heater, the back of his neck prickled. Something felt off. He peered into the shadows behind the heater, his eyes adjusting to the darkness. There, huddled in a dark corner, was a young woman, her eyes wide with fear.

"Lily?" Dom breathed, his voice filled with a mixture of relief and disbelief. His first instinct was that Taylor had kidnapped her, and a rush of anger mixed with concern flooded through him.

Lily flinched, her body trembling. "Please, don't hurt me," she whispered.

Dom's heart ached at the sight of her. He crouched down, softening his tone. "You're safe now," he said, reaching out a hand. "We're here to help you."

Lily hesitated before inching closer, her eyes darting around as if expecting danger to leap from the shadows. Dom kept his voice calm and reassuring. "It's okay, Lily. Taylor's not here. You're safe with us."

She took his hand, her grip weak but desperate. As he helped her to her feet, he glanced back at Lauren, who was standing guard.

Lauren stepped forward, her voice steady. "We need to get her out of here, Dom."

"We will. Let's move." Together, they guided Lily out of the dark corner, the oppressiveness of the room lifting as they moved toward safety.

"Lauren, head upstairs and apprehend Taylor. Get her to the station," Dom instructed. "I need to talk to Lily alone."

Lauren's expression was resolute. She headed back upstairs, leaving Dom and Lily alone in the basement.

Dom turned his attention to Lily, who looked bewildered and scared, but coherent. "Lily, can you tell me what happened? Did Taylor kidnap you? Are you hurt?"

Lily blinked at the barrage of questions and swallowed hard, her voice trembling. "I wasn't kidnapped. I ran away. I wanted to drop out of college, but my parents wouldn't let me. After Taylor reported me missing, I thought my parents would eventually give up. I... I felt like such a failure."

Dom listened, but something about her story felt off. Her demeanor, her hesitation—certain details didn't add up. He took a risk. "I have to admit something—I saw you when you reached out through the mirrors. I can't explain this to the other cops, but sometimes I have a sixth sense... How did you connect with me?"

For the briefest moment, Lily's expression changed before reverting to distress. "I... I don't know what you mean," she sniffled. "I really just ran away."

Dom maintained a neutral expression. "I see. Well, sometimes I'm wrong."

This seemed to placate her, but something was strange about the situation. "Lily, hiding here seems extreme. Are you sure that's the entire story?"

She looked away, biting her lip. "I... I just couldn't handle the pressure. Taylor said I could stay here until I figured things out."

Dom's instincts flared. "Lily, I need you to be honest with me. If there's anything you're not telling me, now is the time."

Lily's eyes filled with tears. "I swear, that's it. I was just scared. I didn't know what else to do."

Dom studied her for a moment longer, his mind racing. He needed to verify her story. "Alright, Lily. We're going to get you somewhere safe. But remember, if there's anything else, we need to know."

As he escorted Lily up the basement stairs, Dom couldn't shake the feeling that there was more to her story. The pieces of the puzzle didn't fit. If Lily was here of her own free will, who was ArdentElan, and why did his IP address point to this house?

Back at the station, Dom and Lauren kept Lily and Taylor separate, aiming to see if their stories aligned. The interrogation rooms were stark and cold, designed to unnerve even the calmest of suspects. Dom sat across from

Lily, a table and a single light between them, casting harsh shadows on the walls.

Dom leaned forward, his expression serious but not unkind. "Lily, we appreciate your cooperation. I need to ask you some more questions, and it's important that you're honest with us."

Lily's eyes were red and puffy from crying. "I understand. I'll tell you everything I know."

"Can you tell me about ArdentElan?" Dom asked, watching her for any signs of hesitation or deceit.

Lily swallowed hard, looking confused but composed herself. "ArdentElan? It's a screen name for an online friend."

Dom kept his gaze steady. "It's more than just a name, Lily. You had very in-depth conversations with him. I believe his name is Luke. Is that correct?"

Lily nodded.

"Did you know if Taylor was involved in anything online?"

Lily hesitated, her eyes flickering with something Dom couldn't quite place. "Taylor didn't talk much about that sort of stuff."

Dom pressed on. "Whose computer equipment was downstairs? Was it Taylor's?"

Lily's eyes narrowed before widening again. "I don't know, maybe it was her dad's before he died?"

"It was on. Someone had been using it," Dom stated, watching her. "It's okay, we have a warrant so we can collect it and figure that stuff out."

"Wait..." She was backpedaling now. "Taylor did her homework on it. Please don't take the computers away. She needs them."

"Oh, don't worry, they will be returned," Dom smiled.

Lily frowned. "None of this is Taylor's fault. I'm not pressing charges. Why can't you leave us alone?" She was shaking now.

Dom lowered his voice, trying to sound soothing. "That's our intention. But a lot of resources were put into this. We want to make sure that everything is okay. You have to understand that we need to look into all angles."

"Yes, of course," her voice was meek and subdued, but strained.

"Lily, this is important," Dom continued. "Did you know Taylor was involved in illegal activities? Did you know she might be ArdentElan?"

Lily's eyes widened with apparent shock that seemed somewhat forced, but Dom could see the wheels turning in her mind. "What? No, I had no idea. Why would she pretend to be Luke? She was just helping me out. I mean, she reported me missing, so my parents would stop looking for me."

Dom noted her reaction, sensing a mix of genuine fear and calculated responses. "Lily, are you sure you didn't know Taylor was involved in something more? Anything about her connection to ArdentElan?"

Tears welled up in Lily's eyes. "I swear, I didn't know. Taylor was my friend. I just wanted to get away from everything."

Dom leaned back, considering her story. It was consistent, but something felt off. "Alright, Lily. Thank you for your honesty. We're going to keep you here for now, but we'll make sure you're comfortable. Do you want anything to drink?"

Lily shook her head.

In the interrogation room, Taylor sat with her hands clasped in her lap, her knuckles white. Lauren stood by the door while Dom entered, his expression unreadable. He took a seat across from Taylor, opening a file and skimming its contents before speaking.

"Taylor, we need to talk about Lily," Dom began, his voice calm but firm. "Can you explain why she was in your basement?"

Taylor's eyes darted around the room, her body language defensive. "Lily asked me if she could stay with me after she ran away. She didn't want to go back home."

Dom's gaze sharpened. "So, she came to you on her own? No one forced her?"

"No one forced her," Taylor replied, her voice steady. "She was really upset. She said she couldn't handle the pressure from her parents anymore."

Lauren stepped forward, her tone more direct. "Taylor, Lily was reported missing. Did you have anything to do with that?"

Taylor took a deep breath, her eyes filling with tears. "Lily asked me to report her missing. She thought if her parents believed she was dead or something, they would stop looking for her. She was desperate."

Dom's expression softened, but his voice remained firm. "That's a serious request, Taylor. Why didn't you contact the authorities when she first came to you?"

Taylor's tears spilled over, her voice trembling. "I know, I should have. But she begged me not to. She said she just needed some time to figure things out. I didn't know what else to do. I thought I was helping her."

Lauren exchanged a glance with Dom, then asked, "Did Lily say why she felt so desperate? Why she wanted to go to such extremes?"

Taylor wiped her tears with the back of her hand. "She felt like a failure because she wanted to drop out of college, but her parents wouldn't let her. She thought if she disappeared, they'd eventually give up and stop pressuring her."

Dom leaned in. "Taylor, did you know if Lily had any other plans? Did she mention anything else that seemed unusual?"

Taylor shook her head. "No, she just wanted to hide. She said she needed time to think. That's all."

"We also need to talk about the IP address linked to ArdentElan," Dom began, his voice calm but firm. "We have evidence that points back to your home network. Can you explain that?"

Taylor's eyes darted around the room, her body language defensive. "I don't know anything about that. I've told you everything. Someone must have hacked into my Wi-Fi."

Dom's gaze sharpened. "Taylor, this is serious. We need the truth. Are you saying you have no idea how your IP address got linked to this activity?"

Taylor's breathing quickened. "I swear, I don't know. I didn't do anything illegal."

Lauren stepped forward, her tone more direct. "Taylor, hiding information can get you into more trouble. Is there anyone else who has access to your network? Anyone who might be involved?"

Taylor's eyes filled with tears, and she looked down. "My dad... He controls everything. He has all the passwords. I don't know what he does on the computer. I'm not allowed to ask."

Dom and Lauren exchanged a glance, confusion clear in their eyes. "Your dad?" Dom asked. "Taylor, your father passed away years ago. Are you sure about this?"

Taylor's tears spilled over, her voice trembling. "He... he says it's for my own good. That he's protecting me. But I can't leave, and I don't know what he does. I'm scared."

Dom leaned back, processing the information. This changed the dynamics of their investigation. Taylor's claims about her deceased father suggested a deeper psychological issue. "Thank you, Taylor. We are going to leave for a moment, but you are safe here."

As Dom and Lauren stepped out of the interrogation room, they conferred in hushed tones. "We need to get a psychological evaluation for Taylor," Lauren said, her concern clear. "Her statements about her father indicate possible schizophrenia or another mental health issue. She might believe what she's saying."

Dom thought hard, a hunch building in his mind—something so far-fetched no one would ever believe him. Well, almost no one. He glanced at the door to Taylor's interrogation room. Getting someone to assess Taylor's mental state at least bought him time.

He looked back at Lauren and agreed. "What about Lily? We should do the same for her. It would help determine if the county will press charges against Lily, too. Their stories are consistent, but things still don't add up."

Lauren considered for a moment. "Okay, we'll keep both girls here for further questioning and observation. We can hold them for up to 72 hours without pressing charges, as long as we're continuing the investigation and they're not being detained unreasonably."

Dom watched as Lauren headed off to make the arrangements. He took a deep breath. They were dealing with more than just a criminal investigation—this was something uncanny.

Back in his office, Dom reviewed the notes and reports scattered across his desk. The next steps were clear: they needed to understand Taylor's mental state and verify Lily's story. But he also had something else to do. The unsettling feeling that had been gnawing at him since the beginning of this case—the sense that there were deeper, darker forces at play—needed addressing.

Dom pulled out an old leather-bound journal, the edges worn, and the pages yellowed with age. It was a relic from his early days on the force, a collection of unsolved mysteries and uncanny occurrences that had never quite left him. He flipped through the pages, his fingers tracing the faded ink of past investigations that had always seemed to brush against the supernatural.

He paused at a familiar entry, a case reminiscent of the current one, and felt a chill run down his spine. Dom knew he had to revisit the past to understand the present. He needed to connect the dots, to see if the shadows lurking in the corners were the same as those that had haunted him before.

CHAPTER 22

July 20, 2019

I rarely work the night shift. We are open until 2 a.m., and most of my shift involves restocking. We're not a big-name store that's open 24/7, but a lot of the people who shop here live in the nearby apartments (myself included). Most of the late-night shoppers are high and just want junk food. We don't sell alcohol, or we would end up with a whole different crowd during this shift.

It's different at night. The store feels almost alive in the darkness, the silence broken only by the occasional customer. Mike, the night manager, is back in his office, surrounded by monitors. He has cameras, so if I have any trouble, he'd be out here in an instant. It's nice to know he's there, a silent guardian in the shadows.

The store's fluorescent lights seem to flicker more at night, casting long, unnatural shadows that dance along the aisles. It's just my overactive imagination getting the best of me, but the shadows seem to move on their own, stretching and shifting in ways that make my skin crawl.

We haven't had a customer in hours, and I'm restocking the cereal aisle. It's cathartic work—cutting open the boxes, shelving, and merchandising. The repetitive motions allow my mind to wander to other things. I've been questioning why I'm doing all this crazy stuff. Does it come from a place of curiosity, or am I missing something in my life?

The fluorescent light above flickers again, and I feel a chill run down my spine. I shake it off and focus on my task, slicing open another box. The sound of the box cutter slicing through cardboard echoes in the empty aisle, enhanced by the silence that fills the store.

Working on astronomy with Ava has been nice. Normal, even. I've never known normal. When I went over to my parents the other day for dinner, I had something to talk about that they were interested in.

"Maybe you can be an astrophysicist," my mom had said, already planning my life for me. But it didn't bother me as much as it had in the past. My dad had just sat there with a cheerful face. This was something he could understand more than the paranormal stuff. Something he could be proud of.

I pause for a moment, lost in thought, and that's when I hear it—a soft whisper from the next aisle over. My heart skips a beat, and I freeze, listening. The whispering continues, too faint to make out the words, and the chill in the air is colder than the store's air conditioning could account for.

I force myself to move, my legs feeling like lead as I step towards the end of the aisle. I peek around the corner, but there's no one there. The whispering stops, and the silence is deafening. My breath comes in shallow gasps, and I tell myself it's just my imagination, but the unease lingers.

The store feels more oppressive now, the shadows darker and the silence heavier. Attempting to shake off the fear, I return to my work, though my hands are trembling. Glances over my shoulder become frequent, expecting to see someone—or something—lurking just out of sight. Considering getting Mike crosses my mind, but I decide against it. He would just think I was crazy.

All the cereal containers on the top shelf tip over simultaneously, as if swept over by some invisible arm. I gasp, stumbling back, my heart pounding in my chest. The sound of them hitting the floor echoes, loud and jarring, in the silence. Did I just stack them poorly? Was the manager playing a prank? He knew I didn't work this shift normally. Maybe it was some sort of initiation thing.

"Mike?" I call out, my voice trembling. There's no response. I know he's watching, but he doesn't come out. Maybe he didn't see it. Maybe he thinks it's nothing.

I take a deep breath, trying to steady myself. The cold air of the store feels sharper against my skin, like needles prickling my nerves. I crouch down and start picking up the cereal boxes, my hands still shaking. The fluorescent lights above flicker again, casting erratic shadows that seem to stretch and twist unnaturally. The feeling of being watched is stronger than ever, and I can't shake the sense that something is here with me, lurking in the shadows.

It feels the same as the shadow in my dreams. Luke and I have restarted our lucid dream practice. He thinks it will be helpful with my Fade experiments and the Lake 40 challenge.

He's right. I've gotten better at it. I think I am leaving my body when I do this. We find each other almost every time we make the attempt now. The one place we can't do it yet is the lake—the same one from the challenge. He thought it would be cool to meet there, even if he's never been there and is all the way on the opposite coast. I try to describe it to him in as much detail as I can. Maybe I'll get pictures on another recon.

In the dreams where we meet, the shadow is always there too, lurking just beyond my vision. It goes away when Luke arrives, and he says he cannot sense it. I question if it's just my imagination. The shadow's presence feels so real, so oppressive, like a dark cloud hanging just out of sight, waiting to pounce.

I stand up, the last box back on the shelf. The store feels even quieter now, as if it's holding its breath, waiting. The silence is thick and oppressive, pressing down on me from all sides. I force myself to move, to continue restocking, but the eerie sensation lingers, creeping into my thoughts and gnawing at my resolve. The shadows seem to dance at the edges of my vision, always just out of reach. Perhaps this shadow is trying to reach out to me. Maybe it needs something, or maybe it's trying to tell me something I can't quite grasp.

Just as I'm about to turn down another aisle, Mike emerges from the back office. His appearance is sudden and almost startling in the store's stillness. He glances around, then looks at me with a faint smile.

"Time to close up," he says, his voice breaking the quiet. "Let's lock things down."

I nod, relieved to see another person, but the tension in my chest doesn't dissipate. Together, we walk through the store, turning off lights and securing the doors. The fluorescent lights flicker one last time before going dark, plunging the store into an even deeper silence.

As we finish up, the unease I felt earlier still clings to me. The shadows and whispers have left a mark, a lingering sense of dread that I can't shake. The night's experience has drained me, leaving me exhausted and on edge. I walk home under the dim streetlights, the memory of the night playing over and over in my mind. The store, a place of routine and monotony, had transformed into something otherworldly and unsettling.

When I reach my apartment, I collapse onto my bed, too tired to even undress. The events of the night swirl in my mind, refusing to let me rest. I know I'll have to face those shadows again, whether in my dreams or in the real world. And as much as it scares me, I can't help but feel a pull towards the unknown, a need to uncover the truth behind these shadows that haunt me. I hope in the Lake 40 Challenge, I can chase away these shadows and bring everything into the light.

CHAPTER 23

October 23, 2019

Dom tossed and turned in his bed, the covers tangled around his legs like the grip of some unseen force. His dreams had been relentless, a barrage of memories and fears woven together into a tapestry of dread. Tonight, however, felt different. The air in his room was thick, oppressive, and the shadows seemed to shift and dance with a life of their own.

The dream always started the same way. Dom stood on a desolate, narrow path that stretched into the darkness of the forest. The night was silent, save for the distant, eerie whisper of the wind. An unnatural light bathed the path, casting long, twisted shadows that seemed to reach out toward him.

Each step echoed in the stillness. The ground beneath him felt wrong, as if it pulsed with a dark energy. His breath quickened, heart pounding in his chest. He knew he wasn't alone; the entity that had haunted him since childhood was near.

A faint, chilling whisper threaded through the air, almost lost in the oppressive silence. Straining to hear, each step sent a shiver down his spine as the path ahead warped and twisted, stretching into an endless corridor of shifting shadows. The air grew heavy, pressing against his chest, each breath a laborious effort.

Turning, there it was—the shadowy figure with glowing eyes, hovering just at the edge of his vision. Its presence was overwhelming, a dark aura that seemed to swallow the light. The entity's eyes burned with a malevolent intelligence, fixing on Dom with an intensity that froze him in place.

Trying to speak, to demand why it haunted him, no words came. Instead, a suffocating silence enveloped him, pressing against his eardrums, making his head throb. The entity advanced, its form shifting and amorphous, a mass of darkness that defied comprehension.

Feeling a hand grip his shoulder, Dom spun around, finding himself face-to-face with a twisted version of himself. His doppelgänger's eyes were empty voids, and its skin was pallid, almost translucent. Panic surged through him, and he backed away, his movements frantic and uncoordinated.

The world around him began to warp and twist, the corridor of shadows elongating, stretching into infinity. The entity's presence was suffocating, a dark cloud pressing in on all sides. Dom's pulse quickened, and he struggled to breathe, his chest tight with terror.

He was back in the old plantation house where he had first encountered the entity. Strange symbols covered the walls, glowing with a sickly green light. The air was thick with the scent of decay and something far more sinister. His breath came in quick gasps, chest tight with terror.

The entity appeared once more, its form shifting and amorphous. Something gripped his throat, squeezing the air from his lungs. Struggling, vision darkening, the edges of his sight consumed by shadow, Dom felt himself slipping away until a light pierced the darkness.

Lily Chen stepped out of the shadows, face pale but determined. Holding a small, glowing talisman in her hand, its light pushed back the entity's darkness. With a swift motion, she placed the talisman on Dom's chest, and the being released its grip.

It recoiled, its form writhing and contorting as the light from the talisman grew brighter. Dom's breath came in ragged gasps as he reached out to Lily, fingers brushing against hers. The connection felt real, grounding him amid the nightmare.

"Lily," Dom whispered, his voice raw with desperation. "How...?"

Before she could answer, the entity surged forward, its dark tendrils wrapping around Lily, pulling her back into the shadows. Dom lunged after her, his hand closing around the talisman. The darkness swallowed them both, and Dom felt himself tumbling through an endless void.

He awoke with a start, his body drenched in sweat, his heart racing. The room was dark and the oppressive feeling from his dream lingered. He sat up, trying to shake off the remnants of the nightmare. The line between dream and reality had never felt so thin, the boundaries between worlds blurred.

Once, when Dom was young, he had confided in his mémère about the dream. Her reaction was one of grave concern. "Chéri, dat be 'The Stalker,'" she had said, eyes wide with fear. "It's a wicked spirit. You must never speak of it again. Once it latch on, it never let you be." Dom had tried to heed her warning, shoving those dreams down deep, yet still, this stalker found him wherever he went.

As his breathing slowed, Dom glanced around the room, half-expecting to see the shadowy figure lurking in the corners. The silence was heavy, each creak in the apartment amplified in his heightened state of awareness. He swung his legs over the side of the bed, planting his feet on the cold wooden floor, grounding himself in the physical world.

His chest ached. With trembling hands, Dom lifted his shirt and saw a mark in the talisman's shape etched into his skin. The flesh was red and angry, the edges still glowing with a sickly green light. He stumbled to the bathroom, flicking on the light and staring at his reflection in the mirror. The searing imprint was real—evidence of the entity's hold on him and Lily's intervention.

Dom's breath hitched as he touched the wound. This was no ordinary nightmare. The entity had reached out from the depths of the Fade, leaving a physical mark on him. The line between dream and reality had shattered.

As he stared at his reflection, the faintest hint of movement caught his eye. In the mirror, just behind him, the shadows seemed to twist and writhe, forming a shape that sent a shiver down his spine. He spun around, but the room was empty, the shadows now still.

Dom's heart raced as he backed away from the mirror, the mark on his chest throbbing in time with his pulse. He couldn't escape the entity's reach, not even in his own home. The nightmare was far from over.

The shrill ring of Dom's phone cut through the oppressive silence, making him jump. His heart was still racing from the nightmare, and the burn on his chest throbbed in time with his pulse. He glanced at the clock on his nightstand—3:00 AM.

He picked up the phone, squinting at the caller ID. Lauren. A knot of worry tightened in his stomach as he answered. "Lauren? What's going on?"

Her voice came through, choked with sobs. "Dom, it's Natalie. She... it's turned physical. I didn't know who else to call. Can I... can I come stay at your place?"

Dom's concern deepened, his grip tightening on the phone. "Of course, Lauren. Come over right away. You're safe here."

He hung up, a protective feeling replacing the lingering dread of his dream. He straightened up the living room, his mind racing with worry for Lauren.

A few minutes later, a soft knock echoed through the quiet apartment. Dom opened the door to find Lauren standing there, her face pale and streaked with tears. Her eyes were red and swollen, her hair disheveled. She hugged herself, her whole body trembling.

"Come in," he said, stepping aside to let her enter.

Lauren walked in, her movements slow and tentative, as if each step took all the strength she had left. She sank onto the couch, her shoulders hunched, as though the situation had bowed her.

Dom sat beside her, unsure where to start. The silence between them was heavy, filled with unspoken fears and the echoes of his recent nightmare.

"Do you want something to drink?" he offered, knowing they both could use something to take the edge off.

"Yeah, that would be good."

Dom went to the kitchen and returned with a bottle of whiskey and two glasses. He poured them each a generous amount, then handed one to Lauren. She took it with shaking hands, her fingers struggling to grip the glass.

They sat in silence for a moment, the only sound the occasional clink of their glasses. Finally, Lauren spoke. "She hit me, Dom. She hit me this time. I never thought it would get this bad."

Dom felt a surge of anger and protectiveness. He clenched his fists, struggling to keep his voice calm. "I'm so sorry, Lauren. You don't deserve any of this. We will get Natalie help, but you need to stay away from her for now, okay?"

Tears welled up in Lauren's eyes again. She blinked, trying to hold them back. "I just... I don't know what to do. I feel so trapped, so powerless."

Dom placed a comforting hand on her shoulder, his touch gentle but firm. "You're not powerless, Lauren. You're one of the strongest people I know."

Lauren took a deep breath, trying to steady herself. "I don't know how it got to this point. Natalie was always difficult, but... it's like she's someone else. She's become so paranoid, accusing me of cheating every time I have to stay late at work."

Dom's heart ached for her. "It's not your fault. She has to face her own demons. But you can't let her drag you down with her."

They continued to drink; the whiskey numbing their pain and easing their fears. They shared stories, laughed, and bonded over their shared experiences. By the time the bottle was empty, they were both feeling a little lighter, a little more hopeful.

After a while, Lauren asked, "What about you, Dom? You've always been so private. What's your story?"

Dom stared into his glass, the amber liquid swirling as he gathered his thoughts. "It's complicated," he began. "My parents... they died when I was young. They were mixed up in some dark stuff—supernatural things. After they were gone, my mémère took me in. She... she knew about the spirit world, taught me more than I ever wanted to know."

Lauren looked at him, curiosity in her eyes. "The spirit world? You mean like the Fade?"

"It's called different things in different places. I've heard it called the Crossroads, the Veil, the In-Between. Doesn't matter what you call it, it's the same thing. And it's been following me for years." Dom said. "It's this... otherworldly place. A realm where the boundaries between the living, the dead, and the other blur."

Dom hesitated, then continued, "There's this... entity... I'm pretty sure it's what killed my parents. I've been dealing with it ever since. It haunts my dreams. Sometimes I wake up feeling like it's still there, watching. Tonight is the first time it left something physical behind." He lifted his shirt, showing Lauren the mark on his chest.

Her eyes widened. "Dom, that's... that's intense. I didn't know."

"It's been a part of my life for so long. Moving here, I hoped to escape it, but it followed me. It's connected to Lily's case. I can feel it." He paused, struggling to find the right words. "I've tried to shove it down, ignore it, pretend it's not there. But it's always there. It's real, and it's relentless."

Lauren's eyes softened. "We'll figure this out, Dom. Together. We are a team."

He looked at her, grateful for her support. She hadn't laughed at a grown man having nightmares. "I know this sounds crazy, but I'm done hiding from it. I'm done letting it control my life. I need to face it, once and for all."

They sat in silence for a while, the weight of Dom's confession settling between them. Lauren's voice broke the quiet, softer and more vulnerable than before. "Thank you for sharing that, Dom. It means a lot. I feel like I understand you better now."

Dom smiled, feeling a sense of relief. "We all have our demons, I guess. But we don't have to face them alone."

Lauren leaned against him, her head resting on his shoulder. "No, we don't."

She sat up, a sudden realization striking her. "The thing in the lake? Do you think that was your entity?"

The memory of the dream was vivid in Dom's mind. "I do. I tried not to be afraid—pretend it was all in my head—but my dream... tonight... Lily Chen was in there."

"But we found Lily," Lauren said, her confusion clear.

"I know. That's the strange part," Dom replied, frustration creeping into his voice. "I see her with my eyes, but I don't think it's her."

"If it's not her, then who is it?" Lauren asked, leaning closer.

Dom hesitated, the thought gnawing at him. "My thought is kind of out there," he said.

Lauren narrowed her eyes. "Well, spit it out."

"I think it might be Malcolm Mitchell," Dom finally said.

Lauren was silent, her face contemplative. Dom watched her, fearing she would think he was crazy. He braced himself for her reaction.

"I know—it's out there," he added.

"No," she replied, shaking her head. "It's brilliant. And it makes sense," she pondered aloud. "I don't know if it's because I am wasted, but that would be the glue. What if Malcolm didn't drown? What if that entity took him?"

Lauren stood, pacing now. "And he is stuck on the other side because they cremated his body."

Dom felt a surge of hope. "And he can communicate through electronics now, forcing his daughter to find him a new body."

Lauren's eyes widened. "Exactly! And that could explain why Lily was acting so strangely."

Dom nodded, the pieces fitting together. "We need to find out more about Malcolm and his connection to the entity. There might be something we missed."

Lauren's expression turned serious. "Dom, whatever happens, we have to stop this thing. We can't let it hurt anyone else."

"Agreed. Let's confront Taylor. If she's a victim, maybe we can convince her dad that my body would be a better vessel for Malcolm."

"And we'll rescue the real Lily," Lauren added, determination in her eyes.

Dom took a deep breath. "That means I'll have to do the Lake 40 challenge again, but this time on the night of the new moon."

"How are we going to get Lily-Malcolm to come with us?" Lauren asked, worry creeping into her voice.

"We'll have to trick them somehow," Dom replied. "Make them think it's for their benefit. We need to plan this carefully."

"We can do this, Dom. We have to."

Dom glanced at the burn on his chest, a stark reminder of the stakes. "For Lily," he said.

"For Lily," Lauren echoed.

"We can't involve the station," Dom added, his voice low and serious. "No one will believe us, and we can't risk them interfering."

Lauren nodded, understanding. "You're right. If anyone finds out what we're planning, they'll think we're crazy. Or worse, they'll shut us down."

As they laid out their plan, the first light of dawn crept into the room, casting long shadows that seemed to dance with anticipation.

CHAPTER 24

July 23, 2019

Calculus is killing my brain. I thought I was good at math, but this is so hard. My grade is currently a B. I know it's good enough, but I have to improve it, or my parents will stop paying for my apartment and school. The thought of getting loans makes me anxious, and my grocery store salary will not cut it. The pressure feels like a weight pressing down on me, suffocating my enthusiasm for everything else.

I went home for dinner with my parents on Sunday and picked up a few things from my old room. One of them was the watch my Grandpa Wei gave me. As I held it, memories flooded back, filling me with a bittersweet nostalgia. I think it's going to be the perfect offering as a personal item for the ritual! If anyone supports my feelings on this, it would be him.

My grandparents live in Arizona now. It seems like that's where all the old people go. It's way too hot for me there. Grandpa gave me the watch as a graduation gift. He confided I was his favorite grandchild because I loved listening to his stories about ancestor spirits and the things that happened to him back in China.

Grandpa always emphasized the importance of our cultural heritage and its deep connection to the paranormal. He would tell me how our ancestors believed in the power of spirits and their influence on our lives. According to him, the spirits could offer guidance, protection, and even warnings. These beliefs were not just old superstitions, but integral parts of our family's history. His stories, filled with mystical experiences and ancestral wisdom, fascinated me and shaped my interest in the paranormal. He believed that understanding and respecting these spiritual connections was essential for navigating the world.

I remember one story in particular. Grandpa told me about a night when he was young, working late on a project in his workshop. The room was bright, and as he was drafting plans, he felt a sudden chill. When he looked up, he saw a shadowy figure standing in the corner. Instead of fear, he felt a strange sense of calm. The figure, he believed, was an ancestor guiding him. Moments later, an idea struck him that solved a critical problem in his design. He always said it was the spirit's way of helping him.

This watch feels like the perfect item for the ritual. Leaving behind something so meaningful might make the ritual work. I feel that Grandpa's spirit, along with the watch, will protect me and guide me through the Lake 40 Challenge.

The hike is in one week. Ava and I will turn in our project the next week. If nothing else, I will hopefully get an excellent picture of the new moon (although it will probably just be a picture of a dark sky.) I still have a week, but I want to make sure everything is ready. I have my hiking poles and safety gear set by the door with a small day pack. Taylor plans to be back to pick me up the morning after around 6 AM, so I will pack a snack or two in case I get hungry. I am nervous and excited, but right now, more excited.

I do the Fade ritual every morning and practice lucid dreaming every night. If anything, it has gotten more creepy, but I am used to it now. It's like I have a dark shadow friend that follows me everywhere. It almost feels like I am studying it. The eerie familiarity brings a strange comfort, a connection to something beyond my understanding.

Before bed, I pull out my laptop to plan where to meet Luke.

DreamSeeker: Hey! The hike is in one week. I think I'm ready.

ArdentElan: I can't wait to hear how it goes.

DreamSeeker: I can't wait to tell you about it. I have my stuff already set by the door. Taylor isn't coming back until around 6 AM, so I'll pack some snacks. I'm nervous, but mostly excited.

ArdentElan: Sounds like you're prepared.

DreamSeeker: I will. I've been doing the Fade ritual every morning. Still want to meet tonight?

ArdentElan: Of course! Where at?

DreamSeeker: Let's do the sequoias. That's my favorite.

I pause a minute to gather my nerves.

DreamSeeker: I've been meaning to ask... Can we talk on the phone or maybe FaceTime tonight before bed? I'd like to hear your voice for real.

A couple minutes go by before he answers. With each second, I feel more and more foolish. What was I thinking?

ArdentElan: Sorry... I didn't mean to ghost there. A little chaos going on here.

There is another long pause, and I see the message showing that he is typing.

ArdentElan: I have some family things going on. My home life is a little strange. I want to talk, but I would rather plan it when I am alone. Is that okay? I'm sorry.

I'm disappointed, but it makes sense. I realize I know nothing about his life, and I have shared so much about mine.

DreamSeeker: I understand. Maybe we could talk about it at the tree?

ArdentElan: That would be amazing. I love that you are in my dreams every night.

DreamSeeker: I love that you're in mine.

ArdentElan: See you soon...

Part of me just wants to touch him. I was never one of those people who had crushes, but this feels... special.

As I close my laptop, the glow of the screen fades, leaving me in the dim light of my bedroom. The reality of my growing connection with Luke washes over me and mingles with the anticipation of the upcoming hike. Grandpa Wei's watch lay on my bedside table, a link to my heritage and the mysterious world I am about to delve into.

CHAPTER 25

October 24, 2019

The early morning sun cast long, stark shadows across the parking lot as Dom and Lauren pulled into the police station. The air was crisp, a biting reminder of the sleepless night they had endured. Both detectives felt the lingering effects of their late-night drinking session, their heads pounding and stomachs churning with the remnants of whiskey and unresolved tension.

Dom parked the car, and they sat in silence for a moment, gathering their thoughts and steeling themselves for the task ahead. Lauren glanced at Dom, her eyes bloodshot. "Ready?" she asked, her voice hoarse.

Dom rubbed his temples. "As ready as I'll ever be. Let's do this."

They stepped out of the car, the cold air hitting their faces like a wake-up call. As they walked towards the entrance, Dom couldn't shake the feeling of unease that had settled over him since his dream. The memory of the entity's eyes and Lily's pale face haunted him, a persistent reminder of the danger.

Inside the station, the fluorescent lights flickered intermittently, casting a harsh glare on the worn linoleum floors. The air was thick with the stale scent of coffee and disinfectant. Dom and Lauren approached the front desk, where Officer Ramirez sat, bleary-eyed and sipping from a chipped mug.

"Morning, Ramirez," Dom greeted, trying to sound more awake than he felt. "We need to check on Taylor Mitchell and Lily Chen."

Ramirez set his mug aside. "Sure thing, Detectives. They're in separate rooms, as requested. Taylor's in three, Lily's in four."

Dom observed Lily through the one-way mirror. She appeared calm, but had an eerie, detached demeanor. Her eyes were unfocused, staring at nothing in particular, yet there was a sense of awareness in her stillness that made Dom's skin crawl. Lauren stood beside him, her arms crossed and her brow furrowed in concern.

"She's too calm," Dom murmured. "It's like she's not even here."

Lauren's face reflected her worry. "I've seen that look before, Dom. It's like she's been hollowed out. Confronting her might do more harm than good right now."

Dom sighed, his gaze fixed on Lily. "Let's be careful."

They turned their attention to the adjacent cell, where Taylor sat hunched over on the narrow cot, her fingers gripping the edge as if holding on for dear life. Her eyes were wide and filled with a mixture of fear and exhaustion.

"Taylor's a mess," Lauren whispered. "She's barely holding it together. We need to approach her gently, make her feel safe."

"Agreed. We need her to trust us, to believe that we can help her. If she shuts down, we'll never get the answers we need."

They watched Taylor for a few more moments, noting the way her shoulders trembled with each breath she took. It was clear she was on the verge of breaking down.

As they entered, Taylor sat on the narrow cot, her knees drawn up to her chest. She looked up, her eyes wide and filled with a mixture of fear and relief.

"Taylor," Dom said, stepping inside. "We need to talk. Can you come with us?"

Taylor unfolded herself from the cot. She stood, her movements tentative and shaky. Ramirez led them to a small interrogation room nearby, where Taylor took a seat at the metal table. Dom and Lauren sat across from her, their faces drawn and serious.

"Taylor," Dom began, his voice gentle, "we're here to help you. But we need to understand what's going on. I know it must be hard to talk about, but we need the truth."

Taylor glanced at Lauren, then back at Dom. Her eyes were wide with fear and desperation. "You don't understand. No one understands."

Dom leaned forward, his gaze steady. "Believe me, I understand more than you might think. I've seen things. .. experienced things that most people wouldn't believe. Things that logic or science can't explain."

Taylor looked at him, skepticism flickering across her face. "What do you mean?"

Dom took a deep breath, choosing his words. "I grew up in New Orleans. My grandmother, my Mémère, was a spiritual healer. She taught me about the other side, about the things that lurk just beyond our world. I've seen spirits, felt their presence. I've dealt with cases that defied explanation. So, when I say I believe you, I mean it."

Taylor's eyes filled with tears. "You believe me?"

"Yes, I do. And I need you to trust us. Tell us everything. We can't help if we don't know the full story."

Taylor took a shaky breath, her resolve breaking. "It started about a month after my father died. I was devastated, but then the nightmares began. They were so vivid, so real. I would see him, hear him, but he wasn't... he wasn't right. He was darker, twisted."

Lauren leaned in, her voice soothing. "Go on, Taylor. We're listening."

"He started appearing in mirrors," Taylor continued, her voice trembling. "At first, I thought it was just my mind playing tricks on me. But then he started talking to me. Not out loud, but in my head. He told me he needed my help, that he was trapped and could only communicate through me."

Dom encouraged her to continue. "What did he want?"

"He wanted to come back," Taylor said. "He wanted to use someone else's body to return to the living world. He could give them power, knowledge, but he needed someone willing to let him in. Not long after that, he would somehow send me messages on the computer."

Dom leaned in, his brow furrowed. "Do you have any evidence? Anything we can look at?"

Taylor shook her head, tears brimming in her eyes. "No, he made me delete the logs. This happened for some time, and he wanted me to reach out to the old Children of the Veil members to see if someone would let him into their body and they could have the privilege of living in the Fade like him. No one volunteered—so then he had me look for someone else. It was hard. I'm not good at making friends."

Lauren's eyes widened. "And that's when you found Lily?"

Taylor nodded, tears streaming down her face. "He found Lily—he just told me where to go. Lily was so fascinated by the supernatural. She was already researching all kinds of rituals and legends. It was easy to get close to her, to convince her to try the things my father suggested."

Dom's heart sank. "What happened then?"

"Lily got deeper in, and then it was time to drop her off at the hike," Taylor said, her voice quivering. "When I picked her up, it was no longer her. I reported her missing when I was at the grocery store—my dad never knew it was me."

Dom exchanged a worried glance with Lauren before pressing Taylor further. "Taylor, when you say it was no longer her, what do you mean?"

Taylor's eyes darted around the room, as if afraid someone or something might be listening. "Her eyes... they were different. Darker, like they were filled with shadows. She spoke in a voice that wasn't hers, and she knew things—personal things—that only my dad would know. I knew his plan had worked."

Dom and Lauren exchanged a grim look, processing Taylor's words, when Officer Ramirez approached them, holding a clipboard. His expression was serious, but there was a hint of sympathy in his eyes.

"Detectives," Ramirez said, clearing his throat. "The girls are free to go. The paperwork's all in order. I need to process them out."

Dom felt a surge of frustration. "Ramirez, can't you hold them just a little longer? We need more time."

Ramirez shook his head, his voice firm but regretful. "I'm sorry, Dom. You know I can't do that without cause. We've got nothing concrete to keep them here. If you can get me something more substantial, I'll help you out, but right now, my hands are tied."

Dom took a deep breath. "Understood. Give us a minute."

Ramirez stepped back, heading to his desk to fetch the release paperwork. Dom turned back to Taylor, his mind racing. "Taylor, listen to me. We don't have much time."

Taylor's eyes widened, and she leaned in, hanging onto Dom's words.

"You need to convince Lily... or your dad, whoever it is now, that he needs more power. Offer my body. Tell him you can trick me into doing the hike. If he bites, let us know. We'll meet you on the 27th, the new moon."

Taylor's face paled, but she nodded, determination replacing her fear. "I'll do it. I'll find a way."

Dom squeezed her hand. "Be careful. This is dangerous, but it might be our only chance."

Just then, Ramirez returned, a stack of papers in hand. "Alright, Miss Mitchell, let's get this done. Follow me."

Taylor stood, casting one last glance at Dom and Lauren. "I won't let you down."

As Dom and Lauren turned to head back to the car, a cold draft swept through the corridor, raising goosebumps on their skin. The fluorescent lights overhead flickered, casting eerie shadows that danced along the walls.

A faint sound of footsteps echoed behind them, slow and deliberate. They both turned.

Lily was walking down the hallway, her movements almost too smooth, too controlled. Her eyes, once warm and curious, were now dark pools of emptiness, staring straight ahead. She moved past them without a word, her gaze fixed on some unseen point in the distance.

Dom felt a chill run down his spine. "Lily," he called out, his voice steady despite the unease creeping into his gut.

She paused, turning her head to look at him. The smile that spread across her lips was unsettling, a twisted mockery of the cheerful expression he once knew.

"Detective," she said, her voice low and almost melodic. "Enjoying the morning?"

Lauren stepped closer to Dom, her posture tense. "Lily, where are you going?"

Lily's eyes flicked to Lauren, and for a moment, they seemed to flash with something dark and ancient. "Just stretching my legs. It's a beautiful day, isn't it?"

Dom's mind raced. Was Malcom toying with them? He needed to stay calm, to not give away their plan. "Take care, Lily," he said. "We'll see you around."

She chuckled, the sound sending shivers down their spines. "Oh, I'm sure you will."

With that, she turned and continued down the hallway, her steps echoing until she disappeared around a corner.

Lauren exhaled, the tension in her shoulders releasing. "That was... disturbing."

Dom's jaw clenched.

They walked in silence to the car, and Dom couldn't shake the image of Lily's unsettling smile. Each step felt like a countdown, the urgency of their task pressing harder with every heartbeat. Time was running out. He knew the station had to release Taylor and Lily. Without concrete evidence linking them to a crime, their hands were tied. Lily's apparent cooperation and Taylor's lack of direct involvement made it impossible to hold them any longer.

***

Back at the station, Dom sat at his desk, staring at the paperwork in front of him. His mind kept drifting back to the chilling encounter with Lily and the burden they had placed on Taylor. The clock on the wall ticked.

Lauren walked in, a cup of coffee in her hand. "Any news?"

Dom shook his head. "Nothing yet. Just trying to get through this paperwork."

Lauren sat down across from him, her expression tense. "We need a plan, Dom. We can't just wait and hope everything works out."

Dom's thoughts were interrupted by his phone buzzing. He glanced at the screen, an unknown number lighting up the display. His heart raced as he opened the message.

"Lily and I will be there on the 27th. Be ready. -T,"

Dom showed the message to Lauren, and she read it. "It's on. Let's get prepared."

CHAPTER 26

July 28, 2019

I'm working another night shift—I have to stay in management's good graces for the flexible schedule they give me. Tonight moves even more slowly than the last night shift I did. We aren't gearing up for the 4th this time, and tomorrow (today?) is Sunday.

"Hey!" Mike calls from the back office. "What was that hike called that you're doing this week?"

I'm not much of a yeller, so I walk to the back of the store, keeping my eye on the door. Mike has the evening news on. I didn't realize people still watched the news on TV, but he is old.

"Check this out." His face is serious.

A woman is on the screen with police lights behind her. Mike turns up the TV.

"Good evening. I'm Sarah Thompson, reporting live from the Lake 40 Trailhead for North Sound News, where a tragic event has occurred.

Authorities have confirmed the discovery of a body near the entrance to this popular hiking trail. The victim, whose identity has not been released, is believed to have been killed in a bear attack. Local wildlife experts are assisting with the investigation to determine the exact circumstances.

The Lake 40 area, known for its scenic beauty, is now the focus of a joint operation involving the county sheriff's office and wildlife officials. Initial reports indicate the victim was likely alone at the time of the attack. Emergency services were alerted when a passerby noticed unusual activity and called 911.

Captain James Monroe of the Snohomish County Sheriff's Office provided a brief statement:

'This is a deeply tragic event, and our hearts go out to the victim's family and friends. We urge hikers to exercise extreme caution and follow all safety guidelines while in bear country. Our investigation is ongoing, and we will provide more information as it becomes available.'

The Lake 40 Trailhead has been temporarily closed as a precaution. Experts are conducting sweeps of the area to ensure safety. Signs warning of bear activity have been posted, and the public is reminded to travel in groups and make noise to avoid surprising wildlife.

As the community mourns this loss, we will continue to monitor the situation and bring you updates as they come in."

She continues, but I tune her out as a wave of nausea washes over me. I had never considered the implications of wildlife. I had been so caught up in the Fade aspect of it. Was the trail even going to be open by Tuesday?

"You look white as a ghost," Mike says. "You should skip that hike—bears ain't no joke."

I open my mouth to speak, but shut it again. It's important to choose my words.

"I may just choose somewhere else," I lie.

He gives a nod. "It's pretty dead tonight, and I'm caught up on paperwork. You can head out early. Won't even make you clock out."

He can tell I am shaken. Mike is a great guy—if it wasn't so late, I would request this shift regularly so I could work with him more often.

"Thanks, Mike," I reply. "Gonna take you up on that."

He gives me a nod. By the time I log out of everything, it's close to midnight. The walk home is always terrifying at night. Most of the people around are harmless. There is a big opiate problem in the area—but they are all in their own world. It's the drunks and the meth addicts you have to watch out for. Their drug of choice makes them more unpredictable. Many people look down on them, but to me, it's more of a systemic problem that I have not figured out how to fix.

Perhaps I'll learn it in my drug of choice—the Fade. Everyone is escaping to somewhere these days.

When I get home, I call Taylor. I don't even bother texting first because I know she will be awake.

"Hi," she answers.

"Hey Tay," I start. "Bad news. They have the Lake 40 trailhead closed because of an animal attack."

"I heard," she answers.

Her voice sounds strange, like she is there but sleepwalking. Or sleep talking, I guess, since we are on the phone.

"I don't know if I can wait a month for another new moon," I say. "Perhaps the universe is trying to tell me to—"

"No, you have to!" she interrupts.

I don't know what is so special about this ritual to her. None of the other ones have captured her in this way.

"There is not much I can do if the trail is closed," I say.

"I can drop you off a little ways down—no one will guard it at night."

"How do you know?"

"Why would they?" she is exasperated now.

"I don't want to be eaten by a bear."

"You'll be fine," she continues. "Just bring some bear spray."

"I don't know..."

"I need to get some sleep," she says. "Let's talk about it in the morning, okay?"

"Fine."

Her line goes silent, and I pull up Discord on my phone. Luke has probably been asleep for hours, but I message him just in case.

DreamSeeker: You there?

DreamSeeker: Hey—something happened. I'm scared.

DreamSeeker: When you get this, let me know when you will be around. I just need someone to talk to.

It's after 1 am now. The darkness outside feels alive, pressing in on me from all sides. Every creak of the old apartment, every distant siren, every rustle of leaves outside my window seems amplified, carrying a sinister undertone.

The Fade has become my obsession, my escape. It's like a drug, and despite my fear, I know I can't stop. The thrill of the unknown, the pull of the otherworldly, it all calls to me. Even if the trail remains closed, even if the danger is real, I will do the ritual. The shadows may whisper their warnings, but the Fade is a siren song I cannot resist.

CHAPTER 27

October 27, 2019

The night was pitch black, the sky devoid of moon and stars, as Dom, Lauren, Taylor, and Lily-Malcolm arrived at the trailhead. Thick tension hung in the air, with every rustle of leaves and snap of a twig amplified in the night. The forest seemed to close in around them, an almost sentient presence watching their every move. Meeting up had been awkward; Dom was unsure if Lily knew he and Lauren were aware of Malcolm's presence. It turned out she did.

"I wouldn't have pegged you as one so interested in the Fade," Lily-Malcolm said, her voice dripping with amusement.

Dom grunted in response. Each step felt like a step deeper into a nightmare, the darkness around them seeming to pulse with a life of its own. He could feel Lauren's nervous energy beside him, her eyes darting around as if expecting the shadows to come alive at any moment.

As they headed toward the trail, Taylor walked a few paces ahead, her body tense, every movement hesitant. She kept glancing back at Lily-Malcolm.

Dom switched on his flashlight, the beam cutting through the inky blackness, casting shadows that danced with each movement. He glanced at the others, taking in their expressions.

Lauren was steady. She handed Dom a small pack containing essentials—more flashlights, ropes, and a few protective charms from Dom's grandmother's collection. "Stay focused," she said, her voice a low, reassuring murmur. "We'll be here if you need us."

Taylor's hands trembled as she handed a backpack to Lily-Malcom. Her eyes darted around, her breath coming in shallow gasps. Dom placed a comforting hand on her shoulder. "You're doing great, Taylor."

Taylor swallowed hard. "I know. I just... I just want this to be over."

Lily-Malcom stood apart from the group, her posture still. Malcolm's presence was obvious in the way she carried herself, an unsettling calm radiating from her. Her eyes were dark. She smiled, a cold, detached expression that sent a shiver down Dom's spine.

"Ready, Detective?" she asked, her voice a haunting echo in the night.

Dom forced himself to meet her gaze. "Ready as I'll ever be."

Lauren squeezed his arm. "Good luck, Dom. Be careful."

"I will." Part of him screamed out how stupid this was.

He turned towards the trail, Lily-Malcolm following close behind. The path was narrow and uneven, the moonless night making every step a potential hazard. The sounds of the night—rustling leaves, distant animal calls—created a symphony that set his nerves on edge.

Dom led the way, his flashlight scanning the path ahead. The trail wound upward, swallowed by the forest. Silence hung heavy between them, each lost in their own thoughts. His mind raced as he calculated every outcome and potential threat. Showing weakness wasn't an option, not now.

Lily-Malcolm moved with disconcerting grace, as if the uneven terrain posed no challenge. The silence between them was palpable, each step bringing them closer to the ritual site. Dom's heart pounded in his chest.

"Hold up," she paused and called to Dom, who stood ahead, looking out into the darkness.

"Let's cut to the chase," she continued. "I am a lot of things, but stupid is not one of them. You are not planning to give up your body just to explore the Fade. I assume you think you can still help the girl?"

Dom grunted; he did not like Malcolm. "She has a name. It's Lily Chen."

Lily-Malcolm sighed. "You know, I am not all bad. It's why I agreed to this. I never wanted to hurt her. At first, it seemed like a win-win."

"How's that?" Dom frowned. It didn't seem like a win to be trapped in the Fade.

"The Veil... The Fade, whatever you want to call it. In my studies, it all came down to the fact it touched other worlds... other universes and dimensions—like a fabric between time."

"So you wanted to skip the world?" Dom spat. "What about your daughter?"

Lily-Malcolm sighed. "You don't get it at all. I just wanted to see her again. My Evelyn... My wife..."

Dom stopped, letting that comment wash over him. He thought of the loved ones he wished he could see again... his parents, his mémère. Then he snapped back to reality. "That doesn't give you the right to steal someone's body."

Lily-Malcolm froze and narrowed their eyes, not replying.

"We need to follow the steps from here on," Dom said, keeping his tone neutral.

Lily-Malcolm looked at him, the smile still playing on her lips. "Lead the way, Detective. Let's see if you have what it takes."

Dom recited the instructions in his head, ensuring he remembered each step.

They continued up the trail. Dom kept his pace steady, ignoring the whispers and rustling sounds that seemed to follow them.

Past the 1.3-mile marker, Dom's flashlight beam cut through the darkness, illuminating a moss-covered rock with a noticeable crack. He stopped and reached into his pocket, pulling out a small locket that had belonged to his grandmother. He hesitated before placing it inside the crack. His eyes stayed focused on the rock and trail, following the ritual's instructions.

He could feel Lily-Malcolm watching him. Her eyes boring into the back of his head. "You're doing well, Dom. Keep going," she encouraged, her voice mocking.

As they moved forward, Dom's mind raced with thoughts of the unknown and the sacrifices he might have to make. He had always been determined, but this journey was testing his resolve in ways he hadn't expected. After a while, he paused.

Without turning around, Dom asked, "Did you find her?"

"Find who?" Lily-Malcolm responded.

"Your wife, asshole... or did you just make that up?"

"Keep moving," Lily-Malcolm said, her tone unread-able.

Dom clenched his fists, the frustration and fear boiling inside him. He would give up his body to Malcom for Lily if that was what it took. It wasn't what he wanted, but he would accept it. But the uncertainty gnawed at him, but he pressed on, each step feeling heavier than the last.

Just when he thought Lily-Malcolm would remain silent, she spoke. "No, I didn't find her. It was not what I expected."

The admission hung in the air. Dom felt a pang of em-pathy, a brief connection between two souls navigating the darkness for their own reasons. The path ahead seemed even more uncertain, but he knew there was no turning back.

"What did you find?" Dom asked, his voice tinged with curiosity and unease.

"It was waiting," Lily-Malcolm replied, her tone distant and haunted.

"What was?" Dom's frustration bubbled to the surface. "Listen, if we are going to do this, at least help me know what to expect."

"The thing..." Lily-Malcolm's voice quivered. "The dark figure."

"Did it ask you questions?" Dom pressed.

"I ran..." Lily-Malcolm's voice broke.

When they reached the lake, its surface was still, reflecting the darkness of the sky. Dom sat facing the water, his back straight, his eyes closed.

"Now listen," he whispered to himself, blocking out everything else. The night seemed to hold its breath.

An oppressive silence enveloped the lake, an almost unnatural stillness devoid of even the faintest rustle of leaves or distant animal calls. Dom's heart skipped a beat, but he kept his composure, opening his eyes to look into the water. Shadows seemed to shift beneath the surface, but there was no sound, no echo—just a void of silence that was deafening in its intensity.

"It's done," Lily-Malcolm said. "Now, let's finish this."

Dom stood, his body tense, every nerve on edge. He turned and walked away from the lake, taking a deep breath as the reality of what he had done sank in. He had followed the ritual to the letter, and now he had to face whatever came next.

Lily-Malcolm smiled a sad smile. "Well done, Detective. Let's see if this works."

Dom looked around, hoping to see Lily somewhere in the shadows. He did not feel different yet, but Lily-Malcolm's demeanor suggested they had crossed over.

Then Dom felt a strange sensation, as if the world was shifting around him. The air grew thicker, the shadows deeper. He glanced down and saw his own body becoming translucent, ghostly. Lily-Malcolm's form mirrored his own, both of them stepping out of their physical shells, their bodies remaining behind like pale, insubstantial echoes.

The world around them seemed different. Colors were muted, and the forest took on an otherworldly glow. The dark was now infused with a strange, luminous quality, as if they had crossed into a place just out of sync with reality.

In a flash of light, their physical bodies blinked out of existence, leaving only their spectral forms behind. Dom looked over at Lily-Malcom, but it was no longer Lily standing there. It was Malcolm, his true form revealed. His eyes were wide with fear, his face pale and twisted in panic.

"This is not what was supposed to happen," Malcolm muttered, more to himself than to Dom. "The bodies were supposed to stay."

Dom clenched his fists, feeling the tension rise. "What did you expect, Malcolm?"

Malcolm turned to Dom, his face contorted with frustration and fear. "I was supposed to return in your body, and Lily to hers. This... this wasn't part of the plan."

Dom's heart pounded in his chest, he knew Malcoms intent was to take his body, but hearing it set him on edge. "So what now? Are we trapped like this?"

Malcolm's eyes darted around, his panic escalating. "No, no, this can't be. There has to be a way back." He paced, his spectral form flickering with each step.

Dom felt a cold sweat form, despite his ghostly state. "Is this supposed to happen?" he demanded, his voice edged with fear.

"I don't know!" Malcolm snapped, his voice trembling. "Something went wrong. This isn't right. We should still be tethered to our bodies."

Dom's mind raced. He had trusted the plan, albeit reluctantly. Now, the uncertainty and fear in Malcolm's eyes only amplified his own dread. "You have done this once," Dom said, trying to keep his voice steady. "How do we get back, or at least communicate?"

Malcolm stopped pacing, his eyes wild. "There must be a way. We need to find the tether, the connection to our bodies."

Dom took a deep breath, trying to steady his nerves. "And if we can't?"

Malcolm's face fell, the gravity of the situation sinking in. "Then we're lost," he whispered. "At least until some other idiot tries the Lake 40 Challenge."

A chill ran down Dom's spine as the reality of their situation settled over him. He looked around at the shadows closing in and felt a sense of urgency. "We don't have time to waste. Let's find that tether."

Malcolm nodded, his fear giving way. "Agreed."

They moved through the forest, their spectral forms gliding. The darkness around them felt alive, the air thick with unseen eyes watching their every move. As they ventured down the trail, Dom couldn't shake the feeling that they were running out of time, and that the path back to their bodies was slipping further away with each passing moment.

"So you were ArdentElan," Dom said to Malcom. If they couldn't get back to the bodies, at least he could figure out how to get a message to Lauren.

Malcolm's eyes gleamed. "Yes, I was."

Dom's mind raced, and he tried not to think about the fact that Malcom had destroyed Lily's life, manipulated people, all selfish gain. "Why?"

"Survival, Detective," Malcolm replied. "It's all about survival."

"If our bodies are gone, we need to figure out what to do next," Dom said. "Tell me what happened to you last time."

They stood there in silence. Minutes stretched into hours, and hours into what felt like days. The surrounding forest was still, the silence suffocating.

Malcolm's eyes flickered with a hint of recognition. "Yes, of course," he said, his voice softer. "Last time... it was different. A dark shadow thing rose from the lake, as if the shadows themselves had come to life. I panicked and started running, but something felt off. I saw other people, but they didn't see me. It hit me then—I had crossed into the Fade but could still see our world."

Dom listened, his flashlight beam unwavering. "What did you do then?"

Malcolm's eyes held a haunted look as he continued, "I went home. I watched my daughter receive the news that I had died and even attended my own funeral. It was strange seeing them cremate my body. That's when I realized I needed a new one. I waited for someone to perform the ritual, but no one did.

"I followed my daughter around and got the idea when she was on her laptop."

Dom felt a chill run down his spine. "So, you could control her computer?"

"Yes," Malcolm said, a hint of pride in his voice. "It was my only means of interaction. In the Veil, I discovered I could influence electronics. At first, it was just small things—flickering lights, static on the TV. I realized I could manipulate electromagnetic fields. It was like having an invisible hand that could touch anything connected to electricity."

He paused, glancing at Dom to make sure he was following. "It took a lot of practice. I learned to focus my energy on specific devices, causing minor glitches or making them behave strangely. It was frustrating at first, but I got better. Eventually, I figured out how to send messages through the computer. It wasn't like typing; it was more about pushing the right sequences and signals to form words on the screen."

Dom listened while Malcolm continued, "When I saw my daughter messaging a friend, I knew it was my chance. I started by changing the text on the websites she visited, then moved on to sending her direct messages. She was scared at first, but I convinced her it was really me. I explained everything, and she agreed to help. Finding me a new body was my way back."

Dom listened, a tumult of emotions swirling within him. He felt a pang of sympathy for Malcolm's desperation. He imagined Taylor, scared and confused, being convinced to help her father in such a strange way.

"We need to move. Staying here isn't going to help." Dom pursed his lips, processing the information. "Let's make the hike down and find a laptop or a phone. You can show me how to reach out to Lauren."

Malcolm nodded. "Fine."

They walked, the forest feeling more alien with each step. The trees were gnarled, their branches like fingers. The ground beneath them felt insubstantial, as if one wrong step could plunge them into an abyss. Silence oppressed them, a tangible force smothering any sound.

Dom felt watched. The air grew colder, shadows deepened, and the forest seemed to close in, an almost sentient presence observing their every move. After what felt like an eternity, they found a tree with strange markings carved into its bark.

Dom stepped closer, squinting. "They see all," he read aloud.

Malcolm's face twisted with fear and anger. "What does that mean?"

Dom shook his head, a chill running down his spine. "I don't know. But it can't be good."

He glanced at Malcolm, who was growing agitated. "Calm down. Panicking won't help us."

Malcolm glared at him, eyes wild. "Easy for you to say. You're not the one who's been trapped here for years."

Dom felt a surge of frustration. "And whose fault is that, Malcolm? You brought this on yourself."

Malcolm's face twisted with rage. "I did what I had to do. You have no idea what it's like to be stuck here for years at a time, to lose everything."

Dom ignored him, focusing on finding a way out. They found another tree with markings. "No escape," Dom read aloud, dread settling in his chest.

Malcolm's face paled. "We're trapped."

Dom took a deep breath, refusing to despair. "We'll find a way out. We have to."

They pressed on; the forest becoming surreal. Dom felt his sense of self fraying, the boundary between his consciousness and the Fade blurring. He forced himself to focus.

Finally, they reached a clearing with a large gnarled tree with a hollowed-out trunk. Dom stepped closer, unease tightening in his chest.

"Look," he said, pointing.

Malcolm stepped closer. "What?"

There was a flicker of movement in the negative space around them, subtle at first, then more pronounced. Shadows coalesced into a form, dark and dangerous, lurking just beyond perception.

"Do you see that?" Dom whispered.

Malcolm looked around, eyes wide with panic. "There's nothing here, Detective. It's just your imagination, happens a lot here."

But Dom couldn't shake the feeling. The flicker in the shadows grew more intense, a sense of impending doom settling over him.

The darkness surged, taking form.

Dom froze, breath catching. "Malcolm, we need to get out of here. Now."

Malcolm turned, face pale. "What are you talking about? There's nothing here!"

Dom knew better. This was just like his dream. He grabbed Malcolm's arm, pulling him forward.

"Trust me, Malcolm. We need to move. Now."

As they hurried through the forest, shadows shifted and twisted with a life of their own. Dom's mind raced, every nerve on edge, the sense of impending doom growing stronger.

They reached a small clearing. The same figure stood in the center, cloaked in darkness, eyes glowing with an otherworldly light, watching, waiting. Fortunately, it did not see them.

"We need to keep moving," Dom said, voice steady despite the fear. "Stay close and don't look back."

They moved around the clearing without looking back, the sense of danger growing with each step.

Dom's mind raced, and then he remembered the words from the Lake 40 challenge: "Do not make eye contact." His instincts screamed at him to follow this advice. He turned to Malcolm, his voice urgent. "We need to keep moving and don't look back. Trust me."

They continued down the trail, Dom leading the way. He focused on each step, the quiet amplifying the sound of Malcolm's footsteps and ragged breathing behind him. The path twisted and turned, closing in tighter with each step.

The sound of Malcolm's footsteps faltered. Then they stopped, followed by a deafening silence.

Every instinct screamed at Dom to turn back, to help Malcolm, but he forced himself to keep moving. He clenched his fists, nails digging into his palms. He didn't dare look back.

The air grew colder, the surrounding shadows more sinister. The forest itself was alive and hunting. Dom's breaths came in short, panicked gasps, but he pushed forward, step after agonizing step.

Finally, he reached the bottom of the trail. He stood alone. When he turned, his worst fears confirmed. Malcolm was gone.

Dom stumbled out of the forest, the darkness giving way to the dim light of the parking lot. His legs trembled with exhaustion, and his breaths came in ragged gasps. The transition from the malevolent woods to the mundane asphalt felt surreal, as if he had crossed from one world into another.

Ahead, he saw Lauren pacing by her car; her phone clutched in her hand. Nearby, Taylor and Lily clung to each other, relief and fear mingling in their tear-streaked faces. Their whispers of comfort and desperation filled the air, but none of them seemed to notice Dom's arrival.

He moved closer, his steps heavy and slow. A pang of longing hit him as he watched Lily and Taylor. He wanted to call out, to let them know he had made it, that he was here. But his voice seemed to catch in his throat, choked by the weight of the night's horrors.

Lauren looked up, her eyes scanning the edge of the forest, but they passed right over Dom, not seeing him. Her face was filled with worry and exhaustion, the toll of the night clear in her weary expression.

Dom felt an ache in his chest, a profound sense of isolation. He was here, so close, yet unseen. It was as if the forest's presence had followed him, casting a shadow that rendered him invisible to those he cared about.

CHAPTER 28

July 30, 2019

There is a soft knock at the door. I rise from my desk and hear Taylor's voice outside, muffled and indistinct. Maybe she's on the phone, but when I open the door, her phone is nowhere to be seen, and she isn't wearing her earbuds.

"Who were you talking to?" I sound more suspicious than I intend. The shadow has become more prominent over the last day or two, and now it's absent.

She looks at me with glazed eyes. "No one. What are you talking about?"

Taylor is spending the night to help calm my nerves. Tomorrow, after Astronomy, we'll finish packing and prepare. The trailhead is only about forty-five minutes away, but we don't know if it's still closed off from the bear attack.

"How are you?" I ask.

She doesn't answer right away. "Oh... Sorry, I'm fine."

"You don't seem fine."

She just scrunches up her face.

Taylor follows me into the living room, where my gear is spread out on the coffee table. She takes a deep breath, looking at the items with a strange intensity.

"Let's go over everything one more time," she says, her voice tight. She picks up each item, examining it like it's the first time she's seen it. "Flashlight?"

"Check," I say, holding it up. "Extra batteries, too."

"Good," she mutters, setting it down. "What about water? You can't risk getting dehydrated out there."

I nod, showing her the two large water bottles. She inspects them, then moves on to the snacks, the first aid kit, the map, and the compass. Her hands are shaking, and she keeps glancing at the door as if expecting someone to burst in at any moment.

"Are you okay?" I ask, my concern growing. "You're acting really... intense."

She doesn't answer, just keeps checking items off a mental list. "I just want to make sure you're prepared," she finally says, her tone bright. "This isn't a game, you know. People have gotten hurt on that trail."

"I know," I say, watching her. "But you've never been this worried before."

She freezes for a moment, then forces a laugh that sounds hollow. "I'm just looking out for you, that's all. We don't know if the trail is still closed because of the bear attack. Better safe than sorry."

There's something in her eyes that I can't quite place. Fear? Guilt? It's like she's hiding something, and it makes my skin prickles.

"Maybe I should bail on this," I say, feeling a pang of guilt for even suggesting it. "If it's making you this nervous, maybe it's not worth it."

Her reaction is immediate and panicky. "No! You can't bail. You have to do it." She grabs my arm, her grip almost painful. "You've been preparing for this. You need to see it through."

Her sudden flip to insisting I go through with it makes my heart race. "Are you sure that's all it is?" I ask, trying to catch her gaze. "You seem... different."

She avoids my eyes, focusing on the map. "I'm fine," she says, too quickly. "Really, I am. I just want you to be safe. Now, did you pack the emergency blanket?"

"Yes," I say, pulling it out of my bag. "But, seriously—"

"Good," she interrupts, nodding. "That's good. And don't forget the whistle. If anything goes wrong, you need to signal for help."

"Taylor," I say more firmly, reaching out to touch her arm. "What's really going on? You're scaring me."

She finally looks at me, her eyes wide and filled with something I can't quite read. "I... I just have a bad feeling about this. I can't explain it, but I do. Promise me you'll be careful, okay?"

The urgency in her voice sends a chill down my spine. "I promise," I say, squeezing her arm. "But you need to tell me what's bothering you."

She opens her mouth to speak, then closes it again, shaking her head. "Just...be careful," she repeats, her voice barely a whisper.

After a tense silence, Taylor stands up. "I need to go. I have some errands to run."

I watch her, confused and unsettled. "Now? You just got here. Are you still spending the night?"

"Yeah," she says, not meeting my eyes. "I'll be back later. Just... stay safe, okay?"

She leaves, almost fleeing the apartment. Her hasty departure leaves me feeling more anxious than ever about the night ahead. Did she want me to bail?

Alone now, I sit back down at the table and try to message Luke, but he is not there. Taylor's warnings echo in my mind. Her behavior was so strange, so unlike her. What does she know that she's not telling me?

I pull out the ritual steps again, my hands trembling as I read through the ominous instructions. Start at midnight.

Be alone. Walk steadily. Don't look back. The words blur as my mind races with possibilities.

The shadows in the room lengthen and shift, stretching out like dark fingers as the light fades. A sense of being watched grows stronger, pressing down like a weight. The air is thick, almost suffocating, with faint whispers seeming to emanate from the corners of the room.

I take a deep breath, trying to steady myself. Tomorrow is the day. I've come too far to turn back now. Whatever awaits me on that trail, I'll face it head-on. But Taylor's words linger, a haunting reminder of the unknown dangers that might lie ahead.

The apartment feels oppressive, every creak of the floorboards amplified in the stillness. I glance at the mirrors I've been using for the Fade ritual, their reflective surfaces dark and silent. They seem to watch me too, echoing the sensation of unseen eyes tracking my every move.

I double-check my packed bag, the familiar items now imbued with a sense of foreboding. Flashlight, water, emergency blanket—all in place, yet somehow not enough to dispel the creeping dread. The night stretches ahead, full of shadows and whispered fears.

. I reach for my journal, hoping to find some clarity in writing, but the words come slowly, burdened by my anxiety. The boundaries between reality and the unknown have never felt thinner, and I can't shake the feeling that I'm teetering on the edge of something vast and terrifying.

Tomorrow, I will step into that darkness. But tonight, the shadows already feel too close, too real. The sense of being watched, of something lurking just out of sight, wraps around me like a shroud. And in the silence, Taylor's warnings echo louder than ever.

Chapter 29

October 27, 2019

Dom's fingers passed through Lauren's phone like mist, a reminder of his current state. Each futile attempt to interact with the physical world left him feeling more and more like a ghost. Frustration gnawed at him, a visceral sensation that seemed to amplify with each failure. He watched as Lauren scrolled through her phone, her anxious glances towards the forest a testament to her worry. It pained him to see her like this, so close, yet unreachable.

Lauren kept glancing at the trailhead, then turning back to Lily. "Are you sure you were alone when you woke up? There was no one nearby?" she asked, her voice tinged with an edge of desperation.

"I am..." Lily replied, her voice quivering. "I am so sorry... everything is so confusing. There was a man... I kept trying to get him to hear me..."

Lily's tear-streaked face was a mask of sorrow, her shoulders slumped in defeat. Taylor, however, had a hard edge to her expression. Her eyes narrowed with suspicion. The wind rustled through the leaves, carrying with it a chill that seemed to penetrate to their very bones.

"How do I know you are not him?" Taylor began, her voice low and urgent. "How do I know it's really you?"

"Who?" Lily asked, her voice soft. "The man that helped me?"

Taylor scoffed and pursed her lips. The space between them was filled with unspoken fears and doubts.

Lily's eyes widened, her lower lip trembling. "Taylor, it's me. I swear. I don't know how to prove it, but I'm still me." Her voice cracked, and she wiped a tear from her cheek. "I was trapped, somewhere dark and cold. It was... it was like a nightmare, but I never woke up."

Taylor's gaze softened, but she remained guarded. "What do you remember?"

"I remember you dropping me off, and doing the Lake 40 challenge." Lily shuddered, wrapping her arms around herself. "Then at the lake... It was like... like being in a place between worlds. I saw shadows, felt things moving around me. I heard whispers, voices I couldn't understand. It was... it was terrifying."

Taylor's expression wavered, doubt and concern warring in her eyes. "Lily, I want to believe you, but this is all so... strange. How can I be sure?"

Lily looked down, her hands trembling. "I don't know, Taylor. I just... I just know I'm me."

Taylor hesitated, the suspicion in her eyes giving way to a flicker of hope. But before she could respond, Lily's gaze drifted to the car's rearview mirror. Her breath caught in her throat as she saw a familiar figure reflected in the glass.

"That's him," she whispered, her eyes wide with shock. "The man who helped me."

Taylor followed her gaze. "Who? What is it?"

"In the side mirror." Lily's eyes filled with tears. "I see him. He's... he's there."

Dom's heart raced. She could see him! He tried to reach out, his spectral fingers brushing against the glass. For a moment, he felt a connection, a spark of recognition.

"Lily, if you can see me, I'm here. I'm trying to get back to you," Dom shouted, willing her to hear.

Lily's fingers touched the mirror, her eyes never leaving Dom's reflection. Taylor looked between Lily and the mirror, her mistrust fading as she saw the raw emotion on Lily's face. "Lily, if you can see him, then maybe... maybe somehow he's really there."

He tried to shout, to reassure them he was fighting his way back, but his voice was lost in the void. His thoughts raced, trying to remember every detail of the ritual, every word and gesture that might offer a way out. He focused, grasping at the fraying threads of his memories. His grandmother's teachings about the Crossroads, the stories she'd told him about navigating the spaces between worlds.

Malcom had said that the place was a fabric between worlds. The item he dropped could it be an anchor? It hurt to think of Malcom- he didn't like the guy, but no one deserved to be torn apart by a shadow (if that was what happened).

Dom started back toward the trail, giving a quick look at Lauren and the two girls. He could do this. He had to.

He focused on thoughts of his mémère. She had been a guiding light in his life, her wisdom a compass in the tumultuous sea of his childhood. Her gentle voice echoed in his mind, calming the storm of his thoughts. As if summoned by his desperation, he saw her on the path ahead; her form bathed in an ethereal glow.

"Come on, mon cœur, you have little time," she called out, her voice a lifeline in the darkness.

Dom wasn't sure if he was dreaming, but he took a deep breath and broke into a run. "Are you real?" he asked, his voice trembling as he followed her up the trail.

"As real as you are," she answered.

He wasn't sure what this meant, but whatever spirit guided him, he trusted it. Dom pondered the nature of dimensions touching, the thin veils between worlds that his mémère had spoken of in her stories. Could this be a true crossing of realms? Was this an intersection of the Fade and the world he knew? And if he died here, would he find his way to heaven, or be lost forever in the spaces between?

The forest resisted him, every step a battle against the spectral currents that sought to keep him trapped. It felt like moving through molasses, each step requiring immense effort. Trees seemed to close in on him, their twisted branches reaching out like skeletal fingers. The ground beneath his feet shifted and buckled, as if trying to trip him up. The air was thick with the scent of decay; the atmosphere pressing down on him.

Dom forced himself to move forward, focusing on the details of his surroundings, grounding himself in the task at hand. The whispers of the forest grew louder, more insistent, a cacophony of sinister murmurs that gnawed at his sanity. He gritted his teeth, pushing the fear aside, concentrating on the path ahead. He could hear the faint rustling of leaves, the distant call of an owl, sounds that seemed to come from another world.

As he ran, his mind wandered to the possibility of an afterlife. If this was a crossing of dimensions, perhaps heaven was just another realm beyond the Fade. His mémère had always believed in a spiritual world interwoven with their own, and now Dom questioned everything he thought he knew. Was his mémère guiding him, or was this a helpful spirit assuming her form to lead him out of danger?

He could almost feel her touch, a gentle push urging him forward. Her presence was a light in the gloom, but doubt lingered. If he died here, would he cease to exist or just remain trapped in this twilight existence? The thought chilled him, but all he could think of was to follow the guidance he was given.

When he arrived at the rock, the ground beneath him seemed to pulse with energy, each step sending ripples through the fabric of reality. His hand reached out, trembling, and felt the cool metal of the locket inside the crack. As his fingers closed around it, a jolt of energy surged through him, grounding him in the physical world. He took a deep breath, focusing on the connection the locket provided.

He looked at his mémère and paused. Part of him wanted to stay with her—he missed the unconditional love she had always given. But this was not his place, and he didn't even know if it was her. "I love you," he whispered. "Send my love to Mama and Papa."

The ground beneath him pulsed with energy, the boundary between the worlds thinning. Dom felt a tug, a pull towards the real world, and he clung to the charm, using it as his anchor. The surrounding forest blurred, and the air crackled with energy, the very fabric of reality shifting.

He could feel the malevolent presences that were just out of reach growing more agitated, the air crackling with its fury. The whispers of the forest became a roar, but Dom's grip on the locket tightened, his focus unwavering. The light intensified, the boundary between worlds becoming more and more tenuous.

He saw his mémère blow him a kiss. There was a blinding flash, and Dom felt himself being pulled through the veil. The sensation was disorienting, as if his entire being was being torn apart and reassembled. The spectral world around him seemed to shatter, the darkness receding in shards of light as the real world came into focus.

He gasped, feeling the cold, damp earth beneath his hands, the weight of his physical body once more grounding him. The transition was jarring; every nerve in his body screamed with pain as he adjusted to the harsh reality. The air felt dense, the scent of soil and decaying leaves flooding his senses.

Dom lay on the ground, the charm clutched in his hand. He looked up at the sky, clouds parting to reveal the first hints of dawn. The ordeal was over, but was it?

Breathing, Dom reflected on his journey. The dimensions had touched, worlds interwoven in ways he could comprehend. His mind swirled with thoughts of spiritual realms, ancient beings, and the thin veil separating life from whatever lay beyond. For now, he was back, and that was all that mattered.

CHAPTER 30

July 31, 2019

*W*ell, tonight's the big night. I've got a weird mix of nerves and excitement churning in my stomach. Going through the ritual steps one more time, just to make sure I've got everything down. I can't shake off the thought of that bear attack, though; nature has its own dangers, even without supernatural elements. Still, I've come this far and I'm too curious to back down now.

If, for some wild reason, I don't make it back; I hope this journal finds its way to someone. It's been an interesting ride documenting all of this. Guess we'll see how tonight turns out. Catch you on the flip side!

I close the journal and run my fingers over the cover, feeling the texture of the worn leather. This journal has been my companion, my confidant, through everything.

It's strange to think of parting with it, but it feels right. It belongs out there, in the wild, where my story unfolded.

Before I place it in my bag, I decide to check my laptop one last time. As the screen flickers to life, I see a message from Luke waiting for me. My heart skips a beat; he must have left it last night. I know he's not online now, but the message is a comforting presence.

ArdentElan: Hey, just wanted to wish you good luck for tonight. I know you're going to do great, and I'll be thinking of you. Remember to stay safe and take all the precautions we talked about. Can't wait to hear all about it when you get back. Take care.

A smile tugs at the corners of my lips. Luke has always been supportive, even from miles away. I type out a heartfelt response, hoping he'll see it when he logs back in.

DreamSeeker: Thanks, Luke. Your support means the world to me. I'm nervous, but I'm also excited. I've been preparing for this for so long, and now that it's here, it feels surreal. I'll follow all the safety measures and make sure to stay on the path. I'll be careful, I promise. Can't wait to share everything with you when I'm back. Take care, too.

I hit send and stare at the screen for a moment, feeling a mix of emotions. The reality of what I'm about to do sinks in deeper. I close the laptop, knowing that the next time I open it, I'll have stories to tell—if everything goes as planned.

I get up and start preparing for the day. The ritual items are laid out on my bed: flashlight, extra batteries, water bottles, snacks, first aid kit, map, compass, emergency blanket, and the whistle Taylor insisted on. I double-check everything, my hands moving as my mind races.

The morning passes in a blur of final preparations. I check and recheck my gear, making sure everything is in place. Each item feels significant, a piece of armor against the unknown. I glance at the clock; time seems to move both too fast and too slow.

Taylor wakes up around noon, her presence a steadying force amidst my swirling thoughts. We go over the plan once more. Her voice calm but insistent. "Remember, stay on the path. And don't forget the whistle."

"I won't," I promise, trying to mirror her calm. But inside, my nerves are frayed, each new piece of advice adding to the weight on my shoulders.

By the time evening falls, the apartment feels charged with anticipation. The light outside fades, the shadows inside lengthening and twisting. I can't shake the feeling of being watched, a prickle of unease that refuses to leave. I check my gear one last time, my hands trembling as I go through the motions.

Finally, it's time to leave. Taylor gives me a tight hug, her eyes shining with unspoken worries. "I love you," she whispers.

"Me too," I whisper back, trying to sound braver than I feel. "You're a good friend."

She doesn't meet my eyes.

As I step out into the cool evening air, I take a deep breath, trying to steady my racing heart. As we head toward her car, I know the trailhead is waiting; the challenge is waiting. Shadows slither around the edges of the sidewalk, the air thick with an unsettling stillness. Tonight, I'll face whatever lies ahead, armed with my gear, my journal, and a heart full of both fear and determination.

Epilogue

December 6, 2019

Dom sat at his desk, the faint glow of his lamp casting long shadows in the room. Papers were strewn across the surface, case files mingling with personal notes and reminders. The familiar scent of old coffee lingered in the air, a testament to the long hours he had been putting in. He sighed, rubbing his temples, trying to dispel the lingering headache that seemed to accompany him.

He shuffled through the paperwork, double-checking reports and completing documents. His mind wandered to the events of the past few months, the haunting memories of the ritual and the spectral forest never far from his thoughts. But life had moved on, and so had he. There were still mysteries to solve, still darkness to combat, but for now, the world seemed a little brighter.

Outside, the December night was frosty, a light dusting of snow covering the ground. Christmas lights twinkled from the buildings around the precinct, adding a festive touch to the otherwise grim atmosphere. The sounds of carolers drifted through the air, mingling with the distant jingle of holiday music from a nearby shop.

After finishing the last of his paperwork, Dom glanced at the clock. It was almost time to meet Lauren. He grabbed his coat and stepped outside, the cool evening air a welcome relief as he made his way down the snowy sidewalk.

The burger joint was a small, cozy place with a warm atmosphere decked out in holiday decorations. A Christmas tree stood in one corner, its lights twinkling, and garlands adorned the walls. The scent of grilled meat and fries wafted through the air, mingling with the sounds of laughter and conversation. Dom spotted Lauren sitting at a booth near the back, a half-eaten burger in front of her. Natalie sat across from her, sipping on a soda, her eyes bright and clear.

Dom approached with a smile, sliding into the booth next to Lauren. "Hey, sorry I'm late."

Lauren shook her head, smiling back. "No worries, we just got here."

Natalie looked up, her expression sincere. "Hi, Dom. It's good to see you."

"You too, Natalie," Dom replied. He could see the changes in her, the way she held herself with newfound confidence. Therapy had done her good, and the sobriety had brought back a spark in her eyes that had been missing for too long.

They chatted and laughed; the conversation flowing. For a moment, it felt like old times, before the darkness had crept into their lives. Dom savored the feeling, grateful for the small moments of normalcy.

Later that night, Dom stood in his bathroom, the harsh light reflecting off the mirror. He stared at his reflection, a deep frown creasing his forehead. The face staring back at him seemed both familiar and alien. His eyes, once filled with determination and resolve, now held a shadow of doubt.

He splashed water on his face, trying to shake the unease. When he looked up, Mirror Dom stared back, his expression twisted with fear. Dom blinked, and the reflection was normal again. Shaking his head, he turned away.

He brushed his teeth, but couldn't shake the feeling of being watched. He glanced at the mirror again. This time, Mirror Dom grinned, a malevolent smile that sent chills down his spine. Dom stepped back, heart racing, but the reflection returned to normal once more.

Dom felt a chill run down his spine. Which one was the real him? The question hung in the air, unanswered, as the two selves continued to stare at each other in the depths of the mirror.

A dark shadow loomed behind the reflection, its presence menacing and suffocating. Mirror Dom's eyes widened in terror, his mouth opening in a silent scream. The shadow grew, enveloping the reflection, as Mirror Dom's silent scream became audible, a piercing, soul-wrenching cry that echoed through the bathroom.

Dom stumbled back, heart pounding, unable to tear his eyes away from the horrific scene unfolding in the mirror. The shadow swallowed Mirror Dom, the scream fading into a haunting silence. The real Dom stood there, breathless and shaken, the echoes of the scream reverberating in his mind.

He took a deep breath, trying to steady his racing thoughts. The road ahead was still uncertain, filled with shadows and mysteries yet to be uncovered. He turned away from the mirror, but the sense of determination that had once guided him was gone. Instead, he felt an overwhelming sense of dread, a profound uncertainty about his own identity and the reality he inhabited.

The night was silent, the world outside calm and still. Dom climbed into bed, the echoes of his past and the uncertainties of his future swirling in his mind. As he closed his eyes, seeking solace in the present moment, he couldn't shake the feeling of being trapped, unable to discern if he was himself or just another shadow in the darkness.

ALSO BY

ALSO BY BETH CONNOR:

Hollow City

The Isdralan Chronicles:
Micah and the Candles of Time
Prodigy of Flame
Bridge of Blood and Thornes

Kindred Spirit Mysteries:
The Secret of Misthaven Island
Bridging the Heart
The Curse at White Pines

About the Author

Beth Connor is a weaver of tales, captivated by writing and fueled by a love for storytelling.

Beth's creative pursuits are a reflection of her life philosophy, and she is always searching for new ways to expand her knowledge and understanding of the world. She has a keen eye for detail and a remarkable ability to create vivid, dynamic settings that resonate with her audience.

Beth's talent has earned her recognition as the author of several published works, including the captivating novel "Hollow City" The Isdralan Chronicles Series, and the Kindred SPirits Mysteries, as well as a contributor to many anthologies. Beth is also an accomplished audiobook narrator and the host of the popular podcast, "Crossroads Cantina."

Despite her many endeavors, Beth remains down-to-earth and dedicated to living authentically, true to her passions and values. She resides in the Pacific Northwest with her husband, two children, and canine companions, who bring her boundless inspiration and delight.